TWO MASKS ONE HEART
LOVE TO NO LIMITS

A Novel

JACOB SPEARS

TRAYVON JACKSON

Good 2 Go Publishing

TWO MASKS ONE HEART
Written by JACOB SPEARS AND TRAYVON JACKSON
Cover design: Davida Baldwin
Typesetter: Mychea
ISBN: 9781943686506

Copyright ©2016 Good2Go Publishing
Published 2016 by Good2Go Publishing
7311 W. Glass Lane • Laveen, AZ 85339
www.good2gopublishing.com
https://twitter.com/good2gobooks
G2G@good2gopublishing.com
www.facebook.com/good2gopublishing
www.instagram.com/good2gopublishing

TWO MASKS ONE HEART
LOVE TO NO LIMITS

Jacob Spears and Trayvon D. Jackson

DEDICATIONS

This book truly is dedicated to our beloved family members: Amy McKinney, Chris Hopkins, and Clifford Wallach. I love you all and promise to continue to keep my head up.

~ Jacob Spears

To my mother, Frankie Mae Jackson; my father, Johnny H. Miley; and the woman who pushes me to continue to push this pen. It wouldn't be possible without you, "Latoya Moye." Let's be successful!

~ Trayvon Jackson

ACKNOWLEDGEMENTS

We would like to thank Good2Go Publishing for making this collaboration possible. To all my beloved sisters, Heather, Tabatha, and Jennifer Hopkins, I love you all and will keep my head held high.

~ Jacob Spears

To my family . . . there're so many, so I say to all y'all I love you . . . Queens, Ruckers, Broomfields, Mileys, Wilkins, and Scales.

~ Trayvon Jackson

To our brother and pre-editor . . . thanks, bra Eriese Tisdale (aka Prince Guru)—UBN 2:12, homie.

To those who came to work and made our days worthy for us both: Sergeant Joseph; Deputies Guin, Cranmer, Young, Parks, Pajkuric, and Franklyn; and Corporals James, Tolley, and Polite.

To every brother and sister locked down . . . remember to remain humble, grow, and improve from all aspects.

To our fans . . . continue to rock with us, because the pen don't get tired . . . Never!

Set me as a seal upon thine heart,
as a seal upon thine arm;
for love is strong as death;
jealousy is cruel as the grave;
the coals thereof are coals of fire,
which hath a most vehement flame.

Many waters cannot quench love,
neither can floods drown it:
if a man would give all the substance of his house for love, it
would utterly be contemned.

~ Song of Solomon, 8:6, 7 KJV

P ROLOGUE

"Hell yeah, Daquan . . . beat his ass!" Daquan's girlfriend, Cindy, screamed out. She and a small crowd at the bus stop on 12th Street watched Daquan go at it blow for blow with a notorious street nigga named Tyrone. The quarrel had escalated into an exchange of fist throwing when Tyrone—a dope boy—confronted Daquan about some money that he owed Tyrone's brother. Daquan stood five foot six and had a swarthy complexion. He was what you called a real countrified nigga. He was 175 pounds and had a set of hands on him like Floyd Mayweather, Jr. Tyrone, on the other hand, stood five eight and weighed 205 pounds. He as well had a reputable name in the brawling street fame. But it was unfortunate today as he tried his darned best to defeat Daquan.

In the middle of the road, they both took turns falling from a powerful blow. But both contenders knew that the ground was no place for a victory. At the bus stop, there were a dozen kids waiting for the bus to arrive to take them to school into the city of Atlanta. They were all from Jonesboro, Georgia, which had no high school of its own. They either had to take the trip thirty miles into East Atlanta or drive themselves every day.

"Daquan . . . knock that nigga out and stop playing with him!" Daquan's sister, Shaquana, yelled out. She was the diva of Jonesboro and favored Gabrielle Union, but was more on the thick side from her waist down. She was Daquan's oldest sister by three years.

At eighteen years old and standing five five, no man from Jonesboro—or anywhere in Georgia for that matter—could call himself lucky but one. Her boyfriend was a nerdy black man who'd graduated from Fulton High School years ago and was now finishing up his last year in law school to become an attorney.

"Oh, girl. He got 'em!" Shaquana's best friend, Champagne, exclaimed. She could deceive you as Beyoncé, if you did not pay attention. Champagne was drop-dead gorgeous and stood five five as well.

"Finish him!" Shaquana screamed ecstatically while jumping up and down in exhilaration as Daquan sat on top of Tyrone and pounded him repeatedly with lightning bolt blows.

Tyrone had exhausted himself to a bad position. He tried to shield himself from the rapid blows, but Daquan was still managing to finding access to Tyrone's face.

"Pussy ass nigga! I told you, pussy ass nigga! Huh, huh!" Daquan screamed out ecstatically.

His adrenaline was in overdrive, and his state of mind was psychotic.

Tyrone was defenseless when a couple niggas from the hood pulled Daquan off of him as he lay sprawled out in the middle of the road, bloody and unconscious.

"That's enough, champ. You did ya thang, shawty," an old school cat named Dirk exclaimed as he pulled Daquan away.

"Yo lip bust, Daquan. Go back home!" Shaquana said while holding a wet towel to his lip.

The bus had arrived, but Daquan was heading in the opposite direction, with another victory in the hood, still making him undefeated.

Despite his elation, there was no way he was going to school with a busted lip. Shaquana got on the bus with Champagne and took their everyday seats—#12—along with the others.

"Damn! Yo brother is a straight head-buster, Shaquana!" Champagne said.

"Yeah, he gets it from our daddy," Shaquana retorted.

"When Daddy finds out, Tyrone ass will really be out cold," Shaquana thought to herself, sharing the same prediction as others on the bus, who also left it unsaid.

You just don't fuck with us Clarks and get away with it! Shaquana thought with a smile. For there was nothing in the world that she would rather be than a Clark.

ONE

"Nigga . . . 'em gone! 'Em gone, nigga!" Daquan yelled out ecstatically as he intensively hit the hit sticks on the Xbox 360 controller.

"Never that, young buck!" screamed out his father, Benjamin as he stopped Daquan from running into the end zone on Madden 2016.

"Awww, man!" Daquan exclaimed in disappointment. *I know I have no chance now*, Daquan thought as he sat back down on the leather sofa.

Moments later, like he'd predicted, he went three and out. But he made it worse when he missed the field goal attempt.

"Dad! Why you never let me win, man?"

"Because, when I was coming up, nobody ever let me win. I had to earn everything in life, shawty. And that's the best way to have it, so that way, a nigga can't brag about what he done did for you," Benjamin retorted.

Benjamin was the man in Jonesboro, Georgia, who supplied 75 percent of the hoods in Atlanta and other neighboring cities. He was the cocaine king, and the streets were his. There wasn't a nigga in town who could match his numbers when it came to the dope game. He resembled Birdman from Cash Money Records and had a mouthful of gold like him as well. Their only distinctness was their tattoos, for Benjamin wasn't fond of excessive tattoos, instead having only a couple.

He was married to a gorgeous redbone sista who was able to cease the womanizer in him, despite a couple of baby mommas. Renae was a twin at forty, as of yesterday, and the love of his life. What had her and her sister on the diva team was their striking resemblance to Toni Braxton, from head to toe. Benjamin was forty-four, yet he appeared much younger. Betting that he was only thirty, you'd lose your money. Despite having other siblings from his dad's previous relationships, Daquan was only close to his sister, Shaquana.

"Ben, are you ready to eat?" Renae screamed from the kitchen of their nice, two-story, four-bedroom home.

They had enough money to be suited in an enormous plush mansion, but Benjamin was no fool. He was prudent. He knew that in order to win the game he played, you had to play it safe. Being conspicuous was only a predestined trip to the feds. He had money to wipe his ass with, but the feds wouldn't know the numbers off of tax dollars unless a rat told them.

"Damn, Ben. Can't you hear me?" Renae asked as she stormed into the den with her hands on her hips, obviously agitated.

"Yeah, baby! Let me finishing beating this young buck!" Benjamin answered.

"Y'all and these games!" Renae exclaimed, rolling her eyes before she walked back into the spacious, unique kitchen.

The smell of her delicious fried chicken would wake a dead man from his grave. And both Daquan and his dad were eager to taste her famous chicken. Daquan's favorite football team was the Atlanta Falcons, and he would lose with them all the time against his dad. Benjamin had the Green Bay Packers and was about to select Aaron Rodgers to throw a Hail Mary down field. He hit the necessary buttons on the controller and watched the ball float down field.

"There he goes," Benjamin said, completing the pass. His next play would send him into the end zone. "Aaron Rodgers . . . quarterback sneak," Benjamin said too late for Daquan to stop as his player ran into the end zone.

"What the fuck!"

"Boy, watch your mouth!" both Benjamin and Renae said in unison as Benjamin slapped Daquan on the back of his head. He then walked out of the den and into the kitchen with his wife.

Damn! I can't never beat him, Daquan thought, slouching on the sofa while watching the Green Bay fans celebrate on the flat screen TV.

"I need to smoke one," he mumbled to himself.

* * * * *

"Girl, look at this leopard catsuit. It's Prada," Champagne exclaimed to Shaquana while admiring it. "On

3

sale at the Lenox Mall in Atlanta."

"That shit has too many zeros. 'Pagne, let's go!" Shaquana said, agitated.

She hated bringing Champagne to the mall. She would get so caught up that she'd forget that there was an exit. She was an extravagant person when it came to shopping—unlike Shaquana, who had an enormous closet loaded with updated name brands with price tags still on them. She also had a closet that Champagne was more than welcome to use.

I hate when this bitch does this, Shaquana thought.

"Champagne . . . can we go?"

"Girl, let me see if I could find me something to wear in here. Valentine's around the corner. I can't be half-stepping with Chad," Champagne said.

They were both dressed in blue Prada mini dresses that accentuated their curves, Jason Wu heels, and a black leather and fur jacket.

"Okay, let's go before you piss yourself," Champagne said, seeing the frustration on Shaquana's face.

"Fuck you, bitch! You always acting like you too good to grab something out my closet," Shaquana answered.

"Whatever!" Champagne said, bypassing Shaquana as she was not in the mood for any disputation. She knew the option was always there and that Shaquana loved her like a sister, but her independent attitude had always stood her pride up. And she was flung around in every possible aspect a person could think of. A man would never get the pleasure of opening a door for her.

"So, what's next?" Champagne asked after walking into the parking lot and getting into Shaquana's black-on-black Audi Q7.

"I need to get this hair so Sheka could do it tomorrow."

"What color are you getting?" Champagne asked.

"Bitch, you know I gotta get that Beyoncé," Shaquana responded as she increased the volume on Rihanna's new hit "Work."

"I guess I'll stunt with you," Champagne said, patting her hair softly while looking in the mirror attached to the passenger's visor.

"Girl, don't act like that, 'cause you know that we stepping fly together," Shaquana exclaimed as she got on the interstate on her way back to Jonesboro.

* * * * *

"Yeah, baby! We could definitely do something on the fifth!"

"Okay. Well, I'll put it in our data," the real estate agent said to Benjamin in a seducing sexy voice over the phone.

"Okay . . . lovely," Benjamin said, hanging up the phone with a long sigh. He was in his plush office at his studio. He owned the record label Money Green Records with his right-hand man, Jarvis, who Benjamin had brought up in the game since he was fifteen.

Jarvis was an elegant thirty-two-year-old with a caramel complexion. He stood five foot eight and he had highly intelligent street and book smarts. There wasn't a woman that would turn him down that he could think of. Everything that he learned from the dope game came from Benjamin, who was a father figure to him—and a father that he never had.

"So, what's up with Philly Contractors?" Jarvis asked, sitting on the plush leather sofa in front of Benjamin's ornate desk while buffing his thirty-two gold teeth with a gold rag.

"Looks like they're still reviewing the demo from the last mixtape with T-Ray," Benjamin retorted.

Although he owned his own label, he was also banking from letting many single artists use his studio, where he had a top-dollar engineer under his employment.

"So, what's the deal with Haitian Beny?" Benjamin inquired.

"He was short on two occasions, so I had him terminated. We have better clientele that are always on time," Jarvis told Benjamin.

Beny was a Haitian connect out of Bankhead, who Benjamin supplied with five kilos of cocaine every month. Benjamin knew of Beny's potential to be short, but he dealt with him differently than Jarvis, who had a no-tolerance code on being short. Those who came up short weren't good quality clients in Jarvis's eyes.

"I'll have a talk with Beny," Benjamin said. "Go ahead and renew his contract,"

He glimpsed the sour look of disapproval that appeared on Jarvis's face. But he provided explanation to no man about his decisions, and Jarvis knew well enough to not ever protest his authority.

"Alright!" Jarvis said as he stood up.

"I'll renew him today," he responded, and then quickly dismissed himself from Benjamin's presence.

* * * * *

I hate when he goes over my head like my motherfuckin' word ain't shit! Jarvis thought as he walked out the back door of the studio.

Out in the parking lot, he bumped into Shaquana and Champagne, who were there to see Benjamin. *Head-on with Paradise and Heaven,* he thought as he got closer to them.

"Hey, Jarvis," Shaquana exclaimed while hugging him in a friendly manner.

"What's good, shawty?" he asked. *Damn, this bitch getting more gorgeous every day pass, and she killin' that damn mini dress,* he thought.

"Nothing. We here to see your dad and hear Antron's new hit," Shaquana said.

"Why you so shy, Champagne?" Jarvis asked.

"Boy . . . please! I'm on my phone," Champagne explained to him. Although he was desperate to always get with her, he knew she was off-limits. *When a nigga had the locks, it was hard for anyone to parade on what they desired,* Jarvis thought.

"Well, I'll catch you ladies later . . . okay?"

"Alright. Take care, bro," Shaquana retorted.

7

When he was out of earshot, Champagne broke her silence and said, "Damn! That nigga is a headache sometimes."

"No! He's fine, girl!" Shaquana said.

"I don't see why you won't hook up with him. That's your daddy's right-hand man," Champagne said.

"My point exactly," Shaquana answered.

"Hey, Daquan . . . shawty! Check it out!" screamed Tittyboo, a short and stubby sixteen-year-old drop-out and Daquan's best friend.

Daquan arrived at Tittyboo's house, just pulling up on his beach cruiser bicycle. It was the only place that he would come to smoke "loud" (marijuana).

"What's up, Titty?" Daquan said as he came through the front door of his apartment.

"Man, I got this clown-ass nigga Reco talking 'bout he don't see nobody on that Madden 2016," Tittyboo exclaimed while lighting up a hydro blunt rolled out of a Dutch cigar.

"That nigga must don't know who Daquan is," Daquan said.

There was only one person that could defeat Daquan on Madden . . . and that was his father.

"That's what the nigga don't know. Because I told 'em. He say he's on his way now. Here . . . warm up, nigga," Tittyboo said as he passed the hydro blunt to Daquan, who came and sat down on his leather sofa.

Despite his age, Tittyboo had what was considered by him and Daquan to be a grown bitch with a ghetto-fabulous booty. Shay was a redbone bitch with three kids, at just twenty-three years old. Unfortunately, Tittyboo didn't father any of the kids, even though they were nonchalant when it came to using protection. Tittyboo was a real go-getter and had an atrocious hustle mentality. And that's what paid the bills—his hustling in the dope game.

"So, what he putting up?" Daquan asked Tittyboo, exhaling the smoke from his nostrils.

"Two hundred," Tittyboo retorted as he bagged up a quarter of hydro into a Ziploc bag.

"Well, that's a loss," Daquan said.

"I know. That's right!" Tittyboo said, bumping fists with Daquan.

T wo

It was 12:20 a.m. when Benjamin pulled up to Club Pleasers, a strip club owned by him which attracted women from all over Georgia. If a stripper wanted to collect a nice bankroll, then Pleasers was the place to work. Dressed in his white-tailored Armani suit and Mauri boots, Benjamin walked into the place. Everyone who was looking knew that he owned the place.

"And we have Majik next, coming to the stage to do her thang . . . like every night," D.J. Spine announced to the anticipating and lustful crowd.

Rihanna blared from the massive subwoofers as the ballers prepared to throw their dollars. Majik was Benjamin's favorite among all the other strippers. As he grabbed a bottle of Hennessy from the bar, he turned on his heels to watch the gorgeous diva make her appearance. She came out with lusty strides, wearing leopard lingerie and some black stilettos that strapped around her caramel calves. Majik immediately took the pole and descended downward and upside down doing an air split while simultaneously making her ass cheeks clap together.

"Damn! That bitch is a money maker, shawty!" Jarvis exclaimed as he came up to Benjamin, who was mesmerized by Majik's performance.

"You got every word of that correct, son!" Benjamin answered, taking a swig from his Hennessy bottle while still looking at Majik.

"Our guy from Florida in the back. He's waiting for you!" Jarvis said as he walked away toward the back office.

Benjamin looked at Majik one last time before he made an exit for the back. She was lying on her side, with her long stallion leg extended in the air, revealing her sultry, plump mound.

Damn, I got to taste that baby there, Benjamin thought to himself while looking Majik in her eyes.

Despite his many attempts at trying to lure her into his world, Majik was a hard shell to crack—unlike most strippers. She was straight business and had class for her image. She was at Pleasers to get a check, and not for self-degradation. She had a fetish for men like Benjamin, but if they ever got a chance to hang out, it wouldn't be from the results of Pleasures.

In the back office, at a long, polished oak-wood conference table sat two ol' school niggas in their mid-forties. They were major clients of Benjamin's from Florida. They locked down the areas of Jacksonville to Stuart to Indiantown in Martin County.

"What's good, Spin?" Benjamin exclaimed, outstretching his hand to shake the boss's.

"Good to see you, my nigga. This bitch swole tonight?" Spin asked him, speaking of the club's full capacity.

"It's Friday, shawty, and the money just started piling in. What's good, Big Shawn?" Benjamin asked the second man, who served as Spin's all-around bodyguard.

"Just loving the scenery, I got to admit . . . ," he said with a sigh. "Florida ain't got shit on these strip clubs," Big Shawn exclaimed.

Big Shawn was a huge fellow who stood six eight and weighed every bit of 325 pounds-plus in solidness. He was a retired NFL linebacker who had played for the Chicago Bears. Spin was a small-figured man who stood five four and was no more than 150 pounds. He was a prudent, trustworthy, and loyal business partner, but he was still put to the test by Benjamin.

The door opened and, to no one's surprise, Jarvis came into the room carrying two duffel bags. He set them on the table in front of Spin and Big Shawn.

"It's all there!" Jarvis said, giving Benjamin the validation that every dollar of Spin's money was on time—like always.

"Spin . . . it's always been a pleasure of doing business with you. Shawty . . . let's continue to keep on the same faces, and we shall prosper together," Benjamin said to Spin while sitting on the edge of the conference table.

"Most definitely, Ben," Spin agreed.

"I put an extra four birds (kilos of cocaine) in the cage. Their faith has always been true, so I didn't see any reason to deny the request," Jarvis told Benjamin.

"That's fine. They are more than welcome," Benjamin said.

He knew beforehand that Spin had requested four extra kilos with the six that he was already paying for on front. But in Spin's presence, it was made to look like Jarvis had made the decision without needing Benjamin's approval. So to Spin, one was always two. What Jarvis would approve of, Benjamin would as well. It was Benjamin's strategic way of catching a snake. If a snake could bite one, then he'd bite two. On a narrow perspective, what a snake would do to Jarvis, then he'd do to Benjamin as well.

"So, I guess we will be seeing each other again in a couple of weeks," Spin said, standing and grabbing the two duffel bags.

"Just as sure as a couple weeks could get here," Benjamin exclaimed.

"I appreciate you too, Ben, as the front man."

"You owe that gratification to him," Benjamin said, pointing his finger at Jarvis.

"I appreciate you, son," Spin said to Jarvis.

"Always a pleasure. You take care of us; we take care of you," Jarvis said.

* * * * *

"So what's up with you and your lil' boo thang?" Renae asked her sister, Brenda, who was in the kitchen watching her prepare potato salad for the next day's dinner.

"He seems afraid of Earl," Brenda said.

"Shit! I would too if my mom was dating a nigga my age!" Renae exclaimed, adding more mustard to her recipe.

"I didn't say Earl was afraid."

"And I didn't say that my nephew was scared either. Brenda, girl, we forty years old. That boy ain't nothing but twenty-five."

"With a superb fuck game out this world!" Brenda said with emphasis.

"I guess!" Renae replied.

"So, if Ben was twenty-five today, you wouldn't date him?" Brenda asked.

"Benjamin isn't twenty-five. He's forty-four and married with kids," Renae answered.

"And Jerome is twenty-five and fine as hell!" Brenda exclaimed.

"Okay. Enough of that! Fuck whomever, child . . . Just know that if you searching for love, then be careful."

"I will, Sis. Thank you," Brenda said. "So, what are we doing for Earl's going-away party? I can't believe that he's going to Iraq."

"You and I both," Renae said.

"I was thinking of just cooking over here . . . and bringing momma over."

"Momma and Ben in the same room is not going to work!" Renae said.

"One day they'll put their beef behind them and see how childish that shit is . . . !"

"Umm . . . excuse me! I know she momma, but it's not Ben's fault that his mother-in-law despises him for who he is. Maybe if she stop being so dourly, things could be different," Renae cut in.

"You right, Sis. But he could at least . . ."

"Shut up and try this, because what you are suggesting . . . will never happen!" Renae said, shoving a spoonful of potato salad into Brenda's mouth.

Renae watched her sister close her eyes as she savored the delicious potato salad.

"So, is it good?"

"Sis, you keep putting them crusty ass feet in your cooking, and I know something," Brenda said, causing Renae to explode into laughter.

"Girl, you so stupid!" Renae said while putting a cover over the bowl to store it in the refrigerator.

"Bitch! What you doing? Give me a bowl of it or something before you put it up!" Brenda begged.

"Tomorrow. Your ass don't know how to react when you taste something good," Renae chuckled.

"I can't believe this shit!" Brenda said. "That's so fucked up!"

"No! That young . . . whatever you call him got you fucked up!" Renae said sarcastically.

"Whatever!" Brenda shouted, shooting Renae her middle finger.

Their bond was unbreakable. Renae was the eldest. Together, the twins had come a long way from their struggling days. Ms. Pearl was all they had, growing up without a father. After losing her boyfriend of fifteen years, their mother was now battling to control her own sanity. After learning that she had diabetes at sixty-eight years old, it was a hard pill for both sisters to swallow, when thinking about living without their dour mother.

"Well, good night. I'll see you in the morning," Brenda said as she began walking toward the door.

"I'll be here, Sis. Love you . . . and goodnight too," Renae said, hugging her sister goodnight.

When Brenda and Renae stepped outside, they saw Shaquana and her boyfriend, Donavon, cuddling with each other in the middle of the driveway.

"Shaquana, where the hell is Daquan?"

"I don't know, Ma . . . he probably at Tittyboo's!" Shaquana answered as Donavon held her from behind.

"Hey there, baby!" Renae said.

She thought highly of Donavon being a nice man for her daughter. She saw great potential in him becoming a fine lawyer soon. Her daughter had good taste, though he was on the nerdy side and ingenuous to the streets. He'd never been in trouble with the law—unlike Shaquana who had beaten a girl to a bloody mess at her school once and had to spend a day locked up.

"Shaquana, go get him and tell his ass to get home, because he taking his ass to school tomorrow."

"Mom!" Shaquana called.

"What?"

"There is no school tomorrow. It's Friday!" Shaquana said to her mom.

"Damn, I thought it was! Shit, it feels like a damn Thursday," Renae said.

"Tell Ben to stop letting your headboard fuck with your head when he in them guts," Brenda said, only loud enough for Renae to hear.

"Shut up, bitch . . . and goodnight!" Renae shot back.

"Good night, Sis!" Brenda said as she walked to her conspicuous black BMW.

I guess I'll shower and wait until Ben gets home, Renae thought as she walked back into the house.

"Shawty, if you staying over, you need to call your ol' girl and let her know," Tittyboo said to Daquan, something that he had to always remind him when he stayed over.

Daquan looked down at his Hublot watch and saw that it was nearly 2:00 a.m. "Man, she probably asleep by now," he said, sluggish from smoking hydro. "I'll call my sis to tell her." Daquan pulled out his iPhone and called Shaquana, who picked up on the second ring.

"What Daquan?" Shaquana asked, seeing her brother's picture light up her screen.

"Where are you?"

"I'm getting in bed . . . where your ass should be . . . and you sound high, boy!"

"Shut up! Tell Ma I'm staying over at Tittyboo's. I'll be in tomorrow."

"You better, because we doing something for Earl. He going away to the army."

"For real?" Daquan asked in surprise.

"Yeah, right. Me too!" Shaquana retorted.

There was no way that he was going to miss out on a family get-together. His dad would always pull out the grill and make his fall-off-the-bone ribs.

"I'll be home in the morning, Sis. Good night. I love you," Daquan said.

"Good night to you too . . . and I love you," Shaquana responded before disconnecting the phone.

Next, Daquan called his girlfriend, Cindy, who was a gorgeous Haitian girl with a caramel complexion and a ghetto-fabulous booty, at sixteen years old.

"Hello," Cindy answered on the third ring, sounding like she'd just woken up.

"I'm coming over. Open the door!" Daquan said. "Yo, Tittyboo. I'll be back," he yelled as he hit the door.

T HREE

When Cindy saw Daquan walking up to her big sister, Bay-Bay's, apartment, she opened the door and allowed him inside.

"What's up, baby?" Daquan asked in a whisper, out of respect that Bay-Bay could be sleeping.

"Why you ain't been tell me that you were coming?" Cindy asked, wrapping her arms around his neck and kissing him on his lips.

He was too high to smell the man who she had just kicked out when Daquan warned her that he was coming. At sixteen, Cindy was a real nymphomaniac, unbeknownst to Daquan. She had him wrapped around her finger like a Snickers wrapper. Her fetish was grown men with money, and being that her oldest sister was her legal guardian, since her parents were deceased, she was able to get away with murder.

"How long you staying?"

"I don't know yet," he exclaimed, holding on to her from the back while walking to her room.

The apartment was dark, and the only light came from her TV in her room. With her Pulse perfume lingering in the air, Daquan was unable to smell the scent of sex in the air from her previous visitor. Daquan wasted no time stripping down to nothing and laying on her bed.

Damn, my pussy still on fire! Cindy thought to herself as she watched Daquan stroke his erection.

"Come out them shorts and give me some of that good pussy, shawty!" Daquan said.

Cindy removed her black boy shorts and training bra and climbed in bed with Daquan. She grabbed his dick and skillfully pleased him first with her superb head game.

"Damn, ma!" Daquan moaned aloud, with his hand on the back of her head.

* * * * *

Earl lay on his back on the leather sofa at his mom's house as he listened to the silence of the atmosphere. In two days, he would be shipped off to defend his country in a third-world country. He was elated, as he was anticipating the change of scenery in life. He heard from a lot of old timers about how great the life of a soldier can be. Never leaving Jonesboro—or even the state of Georgia—he was happy to finally have an opportunity to travel throughout the world. He would definitely miss his mom and the cousins, and certainly the delicious cooking that his Auntie Renae prepared. Thanksgiving was his favorite holiday to taste all her many favorite recipes.

Damn, I'ma miss all that good food, Earl thought.

Earl was an athletic, muscular, dark-skinned, six foot four Idris Elba lookalike. When he was gone, a lot of niggas would have a moment of relief. Always being the quiet one of the family bemused a lot of niggas. And every altercation he had with a nigga in the streets resulted in a medical bill. His Uncle Benjamin would always step in and pay the victim to keep their mouth shut. He would always tell Earl that he saw potential in him, but he couldn't figure out where Earl was heading—and neither could Earl.

It was Uncle Benjamin who had made the day more possible than anyone else, Earl had realized.

He wanted me away from the dope game and the streets because he saw potential. If I had a million bucks, I'd owe it to him, Earl thought as he meditated.

He was a strong believer in traveling to other dimensions through meditation, and he sometimes felt like a demigod. His plans for the army would arrange themselves, because he had no clue what would be waiting for him when he got there. Like always when trying to meditate, he drifted off to sleep, and dreamt about the army. He was out on the battlefield again hiding behind a shed with his M-16 rifle firing away—killing his own men.

* * * * *

Waking up in the middle of the night had become common for Shaquana recently. As a child, she was taught not to drink water before going to bed. With her eyes closed and still in a deep slumber, she walked to the bathroom. Almost there, she stopped in her tracks at the muffled sounds of moans—unsuccessful muffled moans.

"Uhh, shit!" she heard her mom moan out.

"What the fuck!" Shaquana exclaimed to herself, shaking her head as she continued on her way.

Pulling her silk pajamas down and sitting on the toilet, she heard the moans intensify.

"Yes, Ben! Yessss!"

It's really time for me to start looking for a place to stay. I'ma too grown to be hearing my mom and dad getting their groove on, Shaquana thought as her body tingled from the relief of pissing.

"One more damn year . . . and school will be history for me," Shaquana mumbled to herself as she stood up and flushed the toilet. She washed her hands and dried them while thinking of her and Donavon's relationship.

I needed a real man to make me scream out like my momma, she thought.

As much as she cared for Donavon, she just couldn't see why their sex seemed so boring to her.

My daddy tells me I have a winner and to keep him. Shit! If he only knew that his little girl had no winner in the bedroom with his son-in-law, Shaquana thought as she got back under her sheets.

Soon Donavon would be a lawyer, and that was the only reason why she chose to keep him in her life. Despite her complaints about their sexual life, she remained loyal and wasn't giving the niggas who could satisfy her any play times on the clock.

He will be the lawyer, and I will be the best cosmetologist, Shaquana thought as she drifted off to sleep.

* * * * *

On the other side of town, Donavon lay in bed with his lover and thought about where his life was heading.

"Soon, I will be graduating law school and have a big law firm waiting to hire me," he said to his lover, who resembled the model and actress Laverne Cox.

"So what are you going to do about Shaquana?" asked his lover, Berlinda, who was a transsexual model from Atlanta, slowly making his way into Hollywood's limelight.

"Like I always tell you, baby, she will be gone before I graduate. My word is my love . . . and I want to you to trust me, okay?" Donavon said as he passionately kissed him on his newly plumped lips.

"Okay, I will take your word, daddy," Berlinda exclaimed, rubbing Donavon on his bare back.

* * * * *

"If you think you're lonely now, wait until tonight, girl!" Benjamin screamed, serenading to the lyrics of Johnny Taylor's old-school hit as he poured lemon juice over the chicken that he had on the grill to get the taste to his liking.

The get-together for Earl's going-away party was jam-packed inside the living room, kitchen, and den, where Daquan held a Madden tournament with his distant cousins and friends. Benjamin and Earl sat outside by the pool with a couple of family members and enjoyed getting intoxicated from the bottles of consistent Heineken. Despite the numerable count of beers that they'd drunk together, both men did a good job of controlling themselves. The old men played dominoes while the older women played the middle-aged women in spades. Ms. Pearl was among the women inside and did a good job at dodging Benjamin.

"So, have you thought about what you want to do once you're there, Nephew?" Benjamin asked Earl, who was sitting at the picnic table next to the large Coleman grill.

"U.C., to tell you the truth, I don't know what I want to get in. I was thinking that I'll know once I get through boot camp."

"Boy, that's the tough part, Nephew," Benjamin said.

"Tell me something I don't know, U.C."

"Well, not too many people can tell you that your uncle served for four years in the army."

"No shit, U.C.!" Earl questioned ecstatically.

"Yeah, it was fun. I got a chance to fuck a variety of women. You name 'em, I banged 'em!" Benjamin exclaimed.

"Did you ever go to war?" Earl asked curiously.

"Naw, Nephew. Serving ain't always about war. So don't go looking for no war. Let the war—"

"Ben! Renae wanna know how long will the chicken be?" Champagne interrupted from the kitchen sliding door.

"Tell her to send out another pan and come get this one. They've been ready!" Ben retorted.

"But yeah, Nephew, go there and show them white folks that will be drilling you constantly that you have more than what it takes to be a soldier."

When Benjamin looked up, he saw Champagne making her way over to him with another pan of marinated chicken.

Damn! This lil' bitch break necks at every step she take, Benjamin thought as he admired Champagne in her black tights and pink blouse.

"Here you go, Ben. And I'm guessing that this will be the chicken that's done," Champagne said, placing the pan on the picnic table.

"Yeah, be careful. That shit still hot, shawty!" Benjamin said, curve-balling Champagne, who intelligently took notice.

"I bet it is!" she replied with a smile.

"Are ya'll good on the ice out here?" she asked, bending over to open the cooler on the ground.

Damn! That bitch is killing them tights, Benjamin thought lustfully.

"Yeah, it looks like ya'll are okay," Champagne said.

"Thank you, Champagne, for helping out," Benjamin said.

"No problem. You're more than welcome to have my assistance, Ben," she replied as she looked into his eyes.

"That's real now," Benjamin said.

"Damn, Earl! Help a bitch out!" Champagne begged, friskily slapping him on his muscular arms.

"My bad, shawty. You know I'm tore up!" Earl exclaimed sluggishly.

25

"Well, never mind!" Champagne retorted, leaving with the cooked pan of chicken.

"Damn, Neph . . . you mean to tell me that you never tried that?" Benjamin inquired.

"Naw, U.C. She too high maintenance," Earl explained, even though Benjamin was already aware of this. She was no stranger to his world. She was just another statistic in his book.

F OUR

When Haitian Beny pulled up to the projects in College Park, the niggas who he had pushing his product came out of the traps individually and brought out to him their re-up, just like always. His main man was a young nigga named T-Zoe, who was only twenty-three years old. He was a stocky, short fella who put fear—as well as hatred—into a lot of niggas' hearts. T-Zoe was 100 percent Haitian and spoke English well, but with a heavy accent. But when talking with Haitian Beny, he would always talk Creole.

When T-Zoe got into the black Suburban, he wasted no time getting down to business. A lot of niggas were hungry, and the beef among them in the hood meant that a nigga was subject to dying any day. And to T-Zoe, he would die trapping if he had to choose.

"What's good, niggas?" Beny inquired to T-Zoe in Creole.

"Money and slumping!" T-Zoe answered.

In the front seat were Haitian Beny's two most trusted bodyguards: Big Funk and Corey. They were both notorious gunslinging men, who got down with Haitian Beny years ago when he had the streets in Georgia on lock. After doing twelve years in a federal penitentiary, only a few niggas were still roaming who could speak of his past. The rest were either dead, or incarcerated with Tom Brady numbers.

Big Funk and Corey were still around, and an old friend had the dope game in his hands now. This left the door open for business. Despite their friendship, it was only to a level of mutual respect. Benjamin wasn't the type to leave a man for dead. He was the type to let you burn your own bridge.

Haitian Beny was in his mid-forties with Benjamin and was well preserved from his incarceration. So he looked more like he was thirty-two rather than forty-five. He stood five six and was on the slim side. He was never a fan of exercising. He was a smooth, pretty-boy Haitian, with a mouth full of gold, and he wore conspicuous jewelry and kept a dope boy knot (wad) in his pockets. It had been two years since his release, and slowly he was formulating a plan to get back on top. He first had to find competition. Looking at T-Zoe, he saw more than enough potential to make him an element to an expedient end.

"So, what's good with letting me catch a front end on this ride?"

"What are you trying to get on front?" Beny asked in Creole at the mention of front.

That means the lil' nigga can handle more than what he get on a regular or shit popping off from the new whip game, Beny thought. To get a new savor to the dope, he had to be distinctive from Benjamin's.

Haitian Beny would break down each kilo and cut it with a formula that no man in Georgia would discover—as well as no one in America. It was made in Haiti and brought up through Miami, where Beny would travel to go get it.

"Man, that new shit speaking new tongues over here!" T-Zoe said.

"So again I ask, what do you need?"

"Let me try eight ounces on this eight," T-Zoe explained.

Beny rubbed his goatee out of habit, as if he was in deep thought. He'd intentionally given T-Zoe a different product from the other niggas to see what results would come back. So far, he was looking good

"I tell you what . . . I will answer that for you before I leave CP—College Park."

"Alright! That's cool, shawty!" T-Zoe responded, grabbing his eight ounces and storing them in a back brace attached to his body.

"I'll be waiting," T-Zoe said before he exited the vehicle.

"What you think, Big Funk?"

"The same thing we all thinking," Corey answered.

"I think shawty need more product, because he making a killing before these niggas could sell a gram," Big Fun replied.

"That's exactly what I was thinking!" Beny exclaimed.

There was no one else asking for front but T-Zoe, because he needed it . . . which meant that the whip game was back, Beny thought.

He had no choice but to give him eight more, knowing it would be double next week.

* * * * *

"So, he actually gave you eight more like that?" T-Zoe's right-hand man, Maurice asked surprisingly.

Maurice was a Drake lookalike who stood six one and wore a low-fade haircut, unlike T-Zoe, who had lengthy dreadlocks that stopped at the center of his back.

"Hell yeah, shawty! We about to lock all these niggas out. So load up on ammo!" T-Zoe explained.

"Fuck them niggas on 3rd. That nigga Chad ain't stopping no traffic!" Maurice exclaimed.

"I'll whack him . . . and that bad bitch of his."

"Hold on now, nigga. I can't let you take Champagne out. That bitch too gorgeous," T-Zoe spoke up.

"Yeah, that is true. Plus, she got that stuck-up-ass homegirl. What's her name? Sha . . ."

"Shaquana, shawty!" T-Zoe corrected him.

"Yeah, Shaquana."

"I hear that she fucking with a nerd-ass cat," T-Zoe said.

"That nigga ain't from the zone. Fuck 'em!" Maurice retorted while lighting up a hydro blunt.

Knock-knock-knock.

"Who the fuck is it?" T-Zoe asked the person at the door to his and Maurice's trap.

"It's Shine, nephew," the baser (crackhead) replied.

"T-Zoe went to unlock the door, already having a couple of rocks in his hand to serve Shine.

"What's good?" T-Zoe asked.

"I need a hundred, neph!" Shine requested, rocking from foot to foot and side to side out of habit. He anticipated getting his crack to smoke, isolated from the rest of the crackheads.

"That shit good, huh?" T-Zoe asked, taking notice that Shine had been back more than his usual once a day.

"Hell yeah, nephew. That shit is so loud. It got to be two trains somewhere around here. I just can't find 'em," Shine said, scratching his chest and gritting his teeth.

"Here! Now go get all them friends of yours off of 3rd and tell them 12th got that good shit," T-Zoe said as he dumped the pieces of crack into Shine's hand and took the crumpled hundred-dollar bill.

Shine's eyes exploded, making him look like Bill Cosby, when he saw that the quantity of crack in his hand was more than what he'd paid for.

"Sitting there looking stupid ain't doing shit!" T-Zoe retorted.

"Oh . . . um . . . nephew. I'm going right now," Shine stuttered

"Man, that shit got these basers out of character!" T-Zoe exclaimed.

"Shawty . . . Shine told you that he heard two trains. He ain't lying. We those two trains coming, and he ain't the only one that seems to hear them!" Maurice exclaimed.

"Nigga, we about to lock CP down, shawty!" T-Zoe said, dapping Maurice up.

Before he could sit down on the sofa, there were more knocks at the door.

"Damn! Who is it?" T-Zoe screamed.

"Pam!" the crackhead answered.

* * * * *

Majik, whose real name was Tameka Rowland, rolled out of her queen-sized bed at 8:45 a.m. She needed to get a lot of things done today, and she was nowhere near feeling energetic.

"Damn, why can't I live bill-free for a change of scenery?" she asked herself, enervated as she walked to the bathroom with nothing on. She needed a nice soothing shower to bring life into her day.

She was working her ass off at three different jobs—two at fast food restaurants, and then the club at night. She was originally from Palm Beach County in South Florida. She moved to Georgia from Stuart for a better life at just twenty-four years old. *Although life seems burdensome, there is no turning back,* she thought while sitting on the toilet taking a piss.

Rubbing her caramel stallion thighs, she felt the soreness in them.

Damn, I danced my ass off last night. This shit is going to kill me, she thought as she stood to flush the toilet.

"Fucking great!" Tameka shouted, frustrated as she saw blood on the toilet paper with which she'd wiped herself.

"Fine time for a bitch period to come on!" she continued as she stepped into the warm shower.

Well, I guess I won't be hitting the club tonight, she thought to herself as the water cascaded down her body. There was no way that Tameka would be able to work the pole while she was on her period. She was making the money

32

at the club rather than the restaurants, so it would hurt her, because nothing but bills were sitting on her kitchen table.

"Damn! This some fuck shit!" Tameka screamed as she washed her pussy. She was only spotting, but she knew how her flood came monthly. "Don't worry, God will provide," she added as her mood fluctuated.

At five eight and weighing 145 pounds, all in her stallion thighs, she was a gorgeous woman, who had left an abusive relationship in Palm Beach. She had packed her things and left without notice. Turning back to return to the same torture would definitely be insane. She had her eyes on a new man, but she would not make the grave mistake of moving too fast. He saw her, and she saw him, at least what he wanted her to see. He was handsome and always made it known that he wanted her. But she refused to let him want her only for a good time.

"I could please myself well, Mr. Benjamin, so don't try me like I'm some type of slut!" Tameka shouted, lost in her own world . . . with Benjamin Clark on her mind.

Our time might come, but never on your time! It'll be on mine, boo! she thought to herself.

F IVE

I make you niggas get that shit right, nigga!
  Get it right, nigga!
  Fuck what you niggas on,
  Bitch, you ain't from my zone!

"Okay, let's break right there, Antron!" the engineering said over the mic to Antron, who was recording his new album titled *Platinum Hearts*.

"Okay, David," Antron replied as he removed the Beat headphones and walked into the engineering booth.

"Man, these motherfuckers get the job done!" Antron exclaimed.

"Tell me about it," David said as he replayed the last recording to him.

Antron was the hot new artist coming out of Bankhead, who Benjamin had just signed to a $4 million contract, something that Antron had never had in his life. So he was compelled to accept anything that looked like a chance. From the blind side, he was only receiving 10 percent of his royalties, making Benjamin's bank increase at a tremendous rate. Unknowing of the loss from being ingenuous to the rap industry, Antron had no clue that Benjamin was ripping him off of some serious cash. And to discuss his contract negotiations with anyone would be a breach of his contract because it was confidential—and only between the manager and client. Antron was only twenty years old and was known as a pretty boy. He was a red-skinned nigga who only weighed 150 pounds and stood five eight.

The women went crazy over him. Despite the opportunity to have any woman that he desired, he remained single. His eyes were on one gorgeous woman who gave him a boost of energy every time he saw her in the booth. Shaquana had his undivided attention—unbeknownst to her. She just wasn't letting down her guard to betray her man, Donavon, for nothing in the world.

"So, when you think we gonna push this shit out?" Antron asked David, who was a white man in his mid-thirties and one of the best sound engineers in Georgia.

Benjamin had lucked up when finding David online promoting himself. The best talent was always overlooked, and that's where Benjamin went to find his engineering.

"Once we master it here, then we'll send it to Philly to let the bigger boys play with it," David responded, taking a pull from his dro blunt.

"Damn, I can't wait for this hit to hit the streets," Antron announced.

"When you and T-Ray gonna hook up? That'll be nice," David suggested.

T-Ray was another hot rapper, who, unlike Antron, knew the fruits of the rap industry too well to sign. So he stayed solo and paid for this studio time wisely. He was from College Park and was the only competition for Antron.

"Man, I don't know! I got to see if he even has the time to lay a track," Antron said.

"Damn, shawty! That bitch know she killing that skirt!" David exclaimed, looking at Champagne's undulations as she walked down the hall toward Benjamin's office.

"Hell, yeah! She is, bra!" Antron retorted.

That means that Shaquana is somewhere close by, if Champagne is here, Antron thought, knowing them like everyone else did. He was elated at the prospect of being able to see her. He was reluctant to return back to recording, because he was now waiting for his secret crush to show up. However, he didn't realize that he'd be waiting forever because she was nowhere around—and today wasn't in favor of his prediction.

* * * * *

Sitting at the table where the unique candles gave off an aphrodisiac, she watched her man eat her delicious steak, lobster tails, buttered potatoes, and fresh green beans. She knew that she'd put her game down good in the kitchen. Whitney Houston's song "Exhale" played in the background from her surround system. Seductively sipping from her half-empty champagne glass, Brenda was ready to take her man to the next level. She had her own Cam Newton lookalike who played in the Canadian Football League. His name was Jerome, and he would soon be a free agent to play for the NFL.

Brenda was mesmerized by Jerome's striking handsomeness, which made her moist between the legs.

"Damn, baby!" Jerome said, wiping his mouth with a napkin. "Your cooking is delicious, baby."

"Thank you, baby. You're more than welcome. This is a wonderful Valentine's Day, and it's intriguing to know that's it's only going to get better," Brenda said in the most seductive way she could, which turned Jerome on.

"Oh, yeah?" Jerome inquired.

"Yes . . . oh yeah!" Brenda responded in a sexy manner, killing the rest of her Dom Pérignon.

"C'mere, ma!" he said as he stood up.

Brenda placed the empty champagne glass down on the table and walked over to her man. He took her hand and walked her to her luxurious fireplace in the den and held her in his massive muscular arms.

"What's so special about today?" Jerome asked.

Brenda's intellect was telling her immediately that he wasn't expecting the ordinary response. She had had twenty years plus to know prudence when she saw it.

"There's nothing special about today, unless you leave me today," she responded.

The feel of his muscular arms wrapped around her. She felt him caress her accentuated curves in her pink Mouret column gown, which gave her a warm feeling of security.

"You've always found the right words to explain a lot."

"And what's a lot?" Brenda asked as Mary J. Blige's "Mr. Wrong" came on.

That's my shit, she thought.

"You and I are a lot . . . and I want to see the fruits of what's a lot. I want an addition of me and you, baby," Jerome said.

Brenda was speechless as a surge of emotion hit her. She clearly knew what he was conveying when he said "addition," she thought. She was forty years old and had protected herself for years from having another child.

She was feeling Jerome unconditionally, but kids were another road to travel on, and a door that she had no intentions on opening.

"Don't stress yourself. We have plenty of time to think things through, baby!" Jerome said as he lifted Brenda's chin to look into her glossy eyes. "You okay?" he asked with concern.

Instead of answering him, she pulled him down to her level and kissed him deeply and passionately. She could only be understood by actions. Jerome picked her up and carried her over to the antique sofa in front of the fireplace.

"Ummm!" she moaned as she unfastened his belt to his black Versace slacks. They tore each other's clothes off in seconds and let their bodies do the rest of the talking.

As he licked and sucked on her erect nipples, she cupped the back of his head in ecstasy from the titillation of his tongue caressing her body.

"Baby!" she moaned out as he slowly licked her body down to her excessive wetness between her legs.

"Ahhh!" Brenda exhaled in ecstasy while simultaneously arching her back when he placed his mouth on her throbbing clitoris.

"Damn, baby!" Brenda exclaimed breathlessly.

The man she had between her legs, for some reason, knew how to open her up completely—something that a man hadn't been able to do to her in years.

Damn it, Jerome! she thought while Jerome made love to her with his tongue.

* * * * *

The candy, balloons, and 14-karat gold XO necklace with a diamond and gold elephant charm were wonderful Valentine's Day gifts for Shaquana.

She lay in the hotel bed listening to Donavon softly snoring while she cuddled her pink teddy bear. Silent tears cascaded down her face. The scenery had more climax than she'd ever feel sexually with Donavon.

I can't believe him. In the midst of him fucking me, he just went soft on me, Shaquana thought as she quietly emerged from bed with nothing on but her flawless caramel skin.

Walking on the rose petals, the smooth silk feeling of them under her feet gave her a warming comfort. The suite was nice with its personal Jacuzzi that angled toward a view of the city of Atlanta. As she descended into the warm Jacuzzi water, she felt like climaxing right there.

"Damn, this shit feels good!" Shaquana exclaimed.

She immersed into the water and then came to sit on the stairs of the Jacuzzi. Shaquana rubbed her erect nipples, and then down with her hand, she felt her throbbing clitoris.

Before she knew what had taken her, she began rubbing on it in a circular motion, intensifying the stimulation.

"Ahhh!" she exhaled in ecstasy as she slid two fingers into her hairless love box.

Damn! This shit feels good. Fuck! she thought as she continued to rub her clit, dipping her fingers inside.

Sliding backward out of the Jacuzzi, Shaquana lay on the surface of the side, with her legs spread apart like an eagle. She then intensified her thrusting and stimulation to her clit.

"Damn!" she moaned out breathlessly. "Fuck! This shit feels good!"

She closed her eyes and let her mind wander.

She wanted to see Donavon pounding her wet pussy deeply, with her legs on his shoulders. But unfortunately, her mind had other intentions. The man that came to her mind was not Donavon. She was letting him fuck her aggressively from the back. He was pulling the tracks out of her Beyoncé weave.

"Damn!" she moaned, going deep as she could with her fingers.

She saw how her ass jiggled when he thrust in and out of her.

"Fuck yeah!" Shaquana moaned again.

She saw him tense up, and knew that he had come to his first load. But he was still dicking her down with his hand on her hips, catching her as she threw her ass back into his strokes. Her body started trembling as she came to her climax.

"Uhhh! Shit! Shit! Jarvis!"

What the fuck! Shaquana thought as her eyes shot wide open. She was in total surprise and in complete shock of her outburst. With her legs trembling and still feeling her climax, she eased back down into the warm water.

I can't believe I masturbated on Valentine's Day . . . with my man in the room asleep.

Jarvis, she thought with a smile on her face.

S_{IX}

Sitting at his oak-wood desk in his office at the studio, Benjamin had a visitor to whom he just couldn't say no. He hated those types but also knew that it was good to have them in his life. He and Beny were good friends, and it was always, "I wash your back, and you wash my back." Being perspicacious to the game, fundamentals came from the man sitting in front of his desk. Haitian Beny wanted a front, and despite his unwillingness, Benjamin was in no position to tell him no.

"Benjamin, I'ma be straight up and call it how I see it, and please don't take it the wrong way," Beny began, pausing to take a swig from his bottle of Zephyr Hills water. "A man does twelve years and returns to the streets under a new era. There was never a time that you've come to me out there in Bankhead and I ever turned you down . . ."

"Listen, Beny. Before you assume a misconception, you have no obligation to explain shit to a man. Yeah, I needed a hand at a time, but when I came, I came with it in my hand every time. When you came home, I frankly told you that you had everything you needed to pick up where you left off. I understand your consideration and prospect of a consolidation, but I didn't get to where I am today with a partner. I got here by myself.

"I will always be glad to help you," Benjamin said to Beny. "Last week, my assistant wanted to suspend your contract, Beny. But I wouldn't let him over my dead body. And that's something you need to pay more attention to. We've always, in my book, been on the same team, Beny."

"Then let's play ball, Benjamin. You know that Haitian Beny going to make that money. So let me. I'm on my dick, Benjamin," Beny said, standing and leaning in toward Benjamin's desk, looking him in his eyes.

Damn, Beny! Benjamin thought.

"I'm getting five bricks at a time. Double that on front, and I'll triple that to clean my face!" Beny said.

"So, you want me to front you ten on five?"

"Ten on five. Correct!" Beny retorted.

Benjamin stood out of his comfortable plush chair and walked over to his office window. He stared out at nothingness, with his back turned partially toward Beny. Benjamin was never the one to turn his back to any man.

You are subject to two factors when turning your back to a man: death and the preparation of death, Benjamin thought.

"You know my expectations, Beny. I build the bridges; only you could burn them," Benjamin said sincerely, bringing music to Haitian Beny's ears.

"I know you too well, Benjamin, to burn any of your business," Beny said concisely as he outstretched his hand to shake hands with the man who would soon regret the conciliation of the front he was giving to the Haitian.

43

* * * * *

When Champagne saw Chad pull up in his new Chevy Impala SS, she smiled and was excited to see him.

Damn, this nigga and that damn sexy smile, she thought.

Chad Davis was a dark-skinned nigga with waves in his head, who resembled the R&B singer Tank. The women were crazed about him, but he only had eyes for one: Champagne. She was his bitch since she was a freshman at Fulton High School. It made her day being picked up at school in his conspicuous purple Impala on 28-inch, custom rims.

"Damn! You actually came, huh?" Champagne said as she got into the fogged out Impala, fanning marijuana smoke out of her face.

"What were you expecting, someone else?" Chad said, kissing Champagne on her sexy, strawberry-lip-glossed lips.

"Damn, you already taste good, shawty!" he exclaimed, licking his lips.

"Boy, stop looking like that . . . like you ready to eat a bitch to death!" Champagne exclaimed with a laugh.

"Maybe I do. What we protesting?" Chad said as he accelerated out of the school zone.

"Naw, baby. I'm not protesting!" Champagne said as she immersed below the dashboard and into Chad's lap.

"You miss me?" she asked as she slid her hands into Chad's sweat pants and grabbed hold of his dick.

"I miss you more than anything," he retorted, staring down at his arousing erection as Champagne stroked him slowly.

Damn, he thought.

"How much you miss me?" she asked, sticking her tongue in his pee hole and squeezing his nuts altogether.

With no words needed to explain, Chad grabbed the back of Champagne's head and pushed her head down on his length.

"Ummm!" she moaned as she sucked on his dick passionately.

"Damn, baby," Chad exhaled in ecstasy at the sweet fellation of Champagne's skillful head game.

As she sped up the pace, Chad had to control himself and try not to wreck his new car on the interstate, on his way to Bankhead. He couldn't wait to get her to his house because he was ready to release thirty-two years of Chad Davis. Hearing her slurp on his dick was music to his ears—music that a lot of niggas couldn't ever claim of hearing. Nor could they dream of having Champagne's lips wrapped around their dicks.

* * * * *

Despite not approving of Benjamin's decision on fronting Beny ten kilos, Jarvis's input meant nothing. He had a job to do . . . and that's exactly where his concern would be. When Jarvis pulled up to the designated location in Bankhead, he always prepared himself for the possibility of anything that could go wrong. He checked the two clips to his Glock .19s and looked ahead inside the Denny's restaurant. It had begun to rain in a heavy downpour when Jarvis emerged from the Suburban and ran inside.

"Damn!" he exclaimed as he came through the doors and shook the rain from his Falcons jacket.

"Sir, welcome to Denny's. Will you be staying or leaving?" a pretty blonde waitress who resembled Jessica Simpson asked.

"Um, yeah. I'll be staying," he answered as he took a survey of the room and looked for whomever he had come to see. "I'll be joining the two men in the back corner. Be sure to bring your number when you come," Jarvis exclaimed in his smooth Keith Sweat voice.

"Um, sorry. But I'm happily married," the waitress said, flaunting her $50,000 diamond ring.

"All you white bitches married and still be ready to suck a nigga dick!" he wanted to say, but his benignity wouldn't allow him to disrespect a married woman.

"Sorry. He must be a lucky man!" Jarvis said, walking off.

"He is!" Behati exclaimed as she watched Jarvis walk off toward the back, where the two big black men were sitting.

"What's good, shawty?" Jarvis said as he approached the table where Big Funk and Corey sat.

"You late, my nigga. What that . . . !"

"Hold on, nigga. Let's not get big headed. I ain't on nobody's clock but mine, nigga," Jarvis said in a feisty tone.

46

Jarvis, who was fearless of the two men who oversized him, was never the one to back down. As well, he had a reputable name when it came to fist throwing.

"My nigga, we could act a fool or do business, whichever one suits you," Corey said, standing up and extending his six-foot-eight and 235-pound figure.

"Nigga, it's whatever!" Jarvis said, pulling back his jacket and revealing his two Glock .19s tucked in his waist.

Big Funk sucked his teeth and said something indiscernible in Creole. Whatever he said caused Corey to reclaim his seat.

"We don't need no problems, unless it's math problems," Big Funk said.

"Man, listen. I'm a tell ya'll this only one time. The next time either one of ya'll challenge me, I'ma do what I do. Jarvis don't see no nigga!"

"Man, let's get the drop, nigga, so we can go. Save all that ra-ra shit, nigga, for the studio, nigga," Corey replied, ready to pounce on Jarvis.

"Man! See me outside, nigga!"

"Let's go!"

"No! Damn it!" Big Funk exclaimed, causing the people in the restaurant to look in their direction and Behati to stop in her tracks. She was on her way to their table; however, when she saw the look on the big man's face, she about-faced.

"I think we all need to just leave now," Big Funk said, walking past Jarvis. Corey followed suit, leaving Jarvis to

47

take the end. When they were outside, all the other patrons sitting in their vicinity exhaled in relief.

"Both of you niggas act like bitches."

"Man, fuck you, nigga! Check your homeboy!" Jarvis exclaimed as he walked to the back door of his Suburban and reached inside to retrieve a black duffel bag.

"You niggas get that money up . . . that's all!" Jarvis said, tossing the bag on the ground in a puddle of water in front of Big Funk's feet.

Big Funk and Corey watched Jarvis get inside the Suburban and leave. Inside the duffel bag were the ten kilos of cocaine.

"Reckless, huh?" Big Funk said, not appreciating how Jarvis had just handled business. Nor did Haitian Beny appreciate it as he was watching the whole scene from inside a black Lincoln town car. He also didn't like Jarvis, but like a real nigga, he wouldn't expose his hand to his enemies—or enemy.

"There was a time for everything. King Solomon said it best!" Beny said to himself.

SEVEN

Tameka hastily prepared herself for work after getting out of the hot, steaming shower. She'd come home from her second job exhausted from being overworked. She slaved in the kitchen scrubbing pots on one job and worked two positions due to a shortage of staff at her first job. When she came home at 10:00 p.m., she committed herself to taking a catnap before going to the club. Unfortunately, she'd fallen into a deep slumber.

"I can't fucking believe this!" she exclaimed, agitated while bouncing on one leg, trying to slip into her Jordans. Looking at the clock on her nightstand, she only became more frustrated. It was 2:00 a.m., and she was supposed to come out on stage two hours ago.

"Okay, let's go, bitch!" she said, grabbing her Louis Vuitton bag and car keys.

She strutted out of her apartment, leaving all the lights on—something that she would soon regret when the light bill came around. When she got inside her Honda Accord, she looked at her iPhone and saw twelve missed calls from her assistant boss, Jarvis.

"Twelve missed calls!" she yelled out. "Un-fucking-believable!" she shouted as she jumped on the interstate on her way to Jonesboro.

"What the fuck is that smell?" she exclaimed ingenuously to the smell of burnt oil. When she saw the oil light flashing rapidly, followed by a knocking sound, she realized that since having the car for months, and focusing on fixing other failures on the car, she had never had an oil change.

I have to get this shit fixed for real . . . before I be walking, Tameka thought as she turned off of the interstate exit and accelerated into Jonesboro.

Three miles off the interstate and she was pulling into the crowded parking lot of Pleasers. She quickly parked and hurried inside the club, hearing Yo Gotti's song "Down in the DM" emanate throughout the serenading club from the subwoofers.

That got to be Destiny on stage, she thought, familiar with her coworkers' likes.

* * * * *

"What the fuck do you mean, I can't go on stage?" Tameka screamed out to her assistant boss.

"Look, Majik . . . the club closes in two hours. You know the rules . . . late and you pay. You'll be dancing and stripping for free, ma. I don't want to do that to you, so to avoid that . . ."

"Man, listen Jarvis . . . I'm dancing and keeping all my shit!" Tameka balked, attempting to walk around him as he stood in her way. *I can't believe this nigga*, she thought.

"You step on that stage, Majik, and your money will be collected and cut seventy-five percent. If that ain't what you want, then please don't step on my . . ."

"Majik! Damn . . . woman! We've been looking for you all night. Are you okay, baby girl?" Benjamin asked with concern, coming through the backstage door.

"Benjamin, I worked two jobs before I could make it here. For some reason today, I intended to only take a catnap, but I overslept. I've been here an hour, and now I'm being told . . ."

"That she will not take the stage without her money being collected and cut seventy-five percent. Just as the policy reads," Jarvis said sternly, never bothering to look at Benjamin, for his decision was already made on cutting Tameka's money.

"Last time I checked, them rules came from you, Ben," Jarvis said.

Power struggle, Benjamin thought.

"How many times has this happened?" Benjamin asked.

"My tardiness . . . ?"

"I'm not talking to you, Majik. Jarvis, how many times has she been tardy?" Benjamin said, looking at Jarvis, who evidently was catching at attitude.

"This is her first time being tardy," Jarvis responded with spitefulness in his voice that neither Benjamin nor Tameka missed.

This nigga got a problem, Tameka thought, as did Benjamin.

"Jarvis, let me handle Majik. I . . ."

Before Benjamin could finish, Jarvis was gone. Tameka and Benjamin watched him strut away doing everything but pout. Benjamin noted that he would have to sit down in private with Jarvis and talk to him about his over-potency problem. It was getting out of hand, and Benjamin had to put a stop to it.

"Majik, sorry for the trouble. I understand your hard-working and overwhelming hustle. But, you know it's policy . . ."

There this nigga go now, Tameka thought, with a frown appearing on her face.

"Majik, I'm not going to hold you accountable for only one damn tardy. Keep your money, but if it happens again . . . this is life. And in life, we accept our responsibilities and consequences. So, try not to be so pugnacious with your boss, if it ever happens again," Benjamin said, with his hands on her shoulders and staring into her eyes.

"You feel what I'm saying, shawty?"

"Yes, Benjamin," Tameka agreed, loving the feel of his hands on her shoulders. When he removed them, she almost told him to put them back. Benjamin pulled out his iPhone from his black Armani slacks and called the DJ.

"Yo, big man. What's up?" DJ Spine answered.

"Get whoever it is off the stage and announce that Majik is next. Spin her five songs!" Benjamin told DJ Spine.

"Ten four, boss!" DJ Spine answered.

"Thank you so much, Benjamin!" Tameka exclaimed, hugging him and kissing him on the cheek.

Majik then heard her name as she hurried out of her sundress to reveal her black satin thong and bra.

"It's time for Majik to get this money!" she said, bouncing her ass cheeks for Benjamin.

Smack!

"Aww! Don't start nothing you can't handle," Tameka said seductively, still feeling the sting of Benjamin slapping her ass.

"Don't let your mouth cash you a bad check," he said, walking off to see her perform.

"When Majik walked on stage, Jarvis stared at her with fire in his eyes. He watched how she and Benjamin eye-fucked each other as she stripped and did her numbers on the pole.

Pussy has always been a man's weakness. Ain't that what you told me, mentor? Jarvis thought as he closely watched his mentor, with envy in his heart.

* * * * *

Renae had finally given up tossing and turning, once she saw that she couldn't find sleep before it found her. She emerged from bed and looked at the clock glowing on her nightstand. It was 4:45 a.m.

Ben should be on his way back from the club now, she thought as she put on a pink Prada robe and walked downstairs to fix herself a cup of coffee. When she made it into the living room, she saw the illumination from the TV, and Shaquana passed out on the sofa.

"Now she have a damn room but choose to bring her ass down here and ruin my furniture," Renae mumbled as she found the remote to the TV to turn it off. Her presence caused Shaquana to stir in her sleep.

At least Renae knew her surroundings, even when she was asleep as she walked into the kitchen. She couldn't wait for Benjamin to come in.

"I need me some dick, and then I'll take my ass to sleep," Renae said as she prepared her Maxwell House coffee.

Benjamin working at a strip club didn't bother her like it would most women. He was a businessman, despite the few times he'd got caught cheating. He was now married, which meant that she had the man. Renae wasn't ingenuous to men's infidelity; she just played her cards correctly, which was one of the main reasons she refused to get a prenuptial when she married Benjamin. She loved him to death but was too prudent to be a fool.

* * * * *

"I can't fucking believe this shit!" Tameka screamed in rage at the revealing of her car not being able to start because of leaving her parking lights on and killing her battery.

She laid her head on her hornless steering wheel and did something that she hadn't done in a long time. She cried. She cried because of how fast shit could go bad when a person was trying to find gravity in their lives. For the most part, she cried because she was alone.

She was startled when two knocks came on her window. When she saw who it was, she wiped her face and rolled down her window.

"Are you okay, ma?" Benjamin asked.

"To be frank, no . . . Ben. I'm having car trouble. My battery is dead," Tameka told him.

"Damn, do you have cables?" he asked.

"No, I never worked on a car, Ben," she answered.

"Shit! And I don't have none myself. I tell you what . . . give me your address, and I'll have the car picked up in the morning. If you want, I'll pay for a taxi or take you myself," Benjamin offered.

"I don't do taxis, so I'll let you take me home, Ben!" Tameka said, cheering up a bit.

Benjamin looked at his Rolex and saw that it was almost 5:30 a.m.

Damn! Renae going to be upset, he thought.

"Come on. Let's get you home," Benjamin said as he helped Tameka out of the car and walked her to his silver Jaguar XJ.

* * * * *

When Renae saw that it was nearing 6:00 a.m. and Benjamin wasn't answering his phone, she became furious and called Jarvis.

"Hello," he answered on the third ring, awaking out of his sleep.

"Sorry to be waking you, Jarvis. This is Renae. Umm. Where is Benjamin at? Didn't ya'll close the club down together like always?" Renae asked.

Damn! Now the nigga need me when going over my head! Jarvis thought. "Renae . . . something came up important, but I promise you that everything is alright. I'll tell Benjamin to call you right away," Jarvis told her. "Hello, Renae!" Jarvis called out to the dead line. He should have known that Renae wasn't going to buy him taking up for Benjamin.

She knew that Benjamin was still fucking around with women despite their marriage. But not coming home was seriously crossing the line. And there wasn't an excuse in the world that could possibly justify him not coming home to her.

Sorry, shawty, but I tried. Whatever coming his way, he probably deserves it, Jarvis thought. He had seen Ben take Majik home himself, and as well, he knew that Benjamin was making a mistake.

56

EIGHT

It was 7:30 a.m. when Benjamin pulled up to the house. Shaquana and Daquan were both gone to school. Looking at the length of his grass, he was disappointed.

Daquan going to make me pound his ass, he thought, being that it was Daquan's responsibility to mow the law. When he inserted his key into the door, he heard the banging of pots and pans in the kitchen.

"Renae," he called out to his wife, getting no answer. He placed his coat on the sofa and walked into the spacious kitchen, where he saw Renae standing at the sink in her robe and with her hair held up in a variety of colored rollers. She was sipping from her mug of coffee. He sensed from her body language her discomfort with his late appearance.

"Hey, baby. Glad that you are home!" Renae turned around with a suspicious smile on her face that was evident to Benjamin.

"C'mere, baby. You don't have to act crazy now," Benjamin said as he slid his hands through her robe and caressed her smooth, flawless red skin. When he kissed her on the lips, all of her anger slowly transformed into pleasure. He knew that he had to assuage her by his love-making.

"Mmmm!" she slowly moaned as he kissed her deeply.

She slowly unfastened his belt and let his slacks fall to the ground. When she grabbed his erect dick, she broke away from his fascinating, hypnotic, passionate kissing and squatted down to her knees.

Being in the game of cheating men, she knew what to look for. She slowly took her tongue and seductively licked him from his scrotum along his shaft. When she tasted no soap or another woman's sexual fluids, she took him into her mouth.

"Damn, baby!" Benjamin moaned as Renae slurped on his enormous-sized love tool.

Benjamin was no fool. He knew his wife well. Bad as he wanted to fuck Majik before coming home, he knew that it wasn't a clever move. The more she tasted only him and no other woman, the more her guilty conscience taunted her, and she intensified her performance.

Before he exploded from her superb head game, she wanted to feel her husband deep inside her. In one swift movement, Renae sprung from her knees and turned around to grab the edge of the sink with her left hand. She pulled her robe over her red ass and wiggled it, swaying from side to side.

"Daddy. Punish me, please! I haven't been a good girl!" Renae begged seductively.

When Benjamin entered her excessive wetness, she moaned in pleasure as she arched her back.

"Yesss, Ben! Yess!" she yelled out, gripping the edge of the sink as he thrust in and out of her deeply and powerfully.

He knew what she wanted and how she felt by questioning his faithfulness.

Benjamin was a fool to be cheating on his wife. *But I ain't no damn fool to get caught twice*, he thought as he pounded Renae's sweet, tight pussy that sent him head over heels every time he was in it.

To Benjamin, there was no woman's pussy greater than Renae's. Despite his cheating, he wouldn't leave his wife for any woman in the world.

"Baby, I love you!" she screamed as she climaxed.

"I love you too, baby," Benjamin retorted, breathlessly moaning every word—genuinely.

Mosul, Iraq

"Down . . . up!"

"One hundred fifty, sir!" the platoon exclaimed in unison.

"On your feet!" the platoon sergeant ordered, bringing his men to their feet. Earl was in the first row, elated that the day was coming to an end. This meant the weekend was about to begin, and the bars would be open all night.

It was his last week in boot camp, and then he would move on to his permanent duty. He was going to the infantry and would be stationed in Ramadi, Iraq, where disaster occurred every day.

"You men will report to your station in another week . . . remember this platoon sergeant's lessons. Every one of you standing in my presence has what it takes to be a soldier. Let's keep it that way!" the platoon sergeant, who was only twenty-five years old but a vicious soldier who had defeated two bomb attacks, said.

"Damn! I'm glad this shit is over!" Earl said to his roommate, Charles Hamilton.

"Hell yeah! What's up? We hitting the Arab bar tonight or what?" Charles asked.

"Shit! You already know. I want to see if I can catch that pretty Iraqi who served us last time," Earl retorted.

Charles was a Mississippi nigga who stood six five and was 225 pounds of solid muscle. He and Earl quickly bonded on the plane ride from Washington to Baghdad and had become the best of homies. The new scenery with the new hospitality of people warmed Earl. He was loving every bit of the new view.

For sure, it was way better than seeing my mom fuck a kid the same age as me, Earl thought as he walked back to the room with Charles.

* * * * *

Haitian Beny was a man to mastermind. The fifty bricks that he'd quickly turned into thirty, from his superb technique when it came to manufacturing cocaine, had him seeing some familiar numbers.

This is only the beginning, he thought as he counted another $100,000. His special whip was dominating every nigga who tried it, including Benjamin, who had no clue of the monster that he'd created.

The niggas in College Park were killing each other to minimize the competition. And like he already knew, T-Zoe was holding his turf down.

There is a drug war going on. When it is done, I'll still be standing, he thought as he sparked up a hydro blunt. He took the $100,000 and placed it inside a duffel bag to be shipped back to Haiti.

If I ever had to do time again, I'd be straight. I have no empathy for no nigga . . . and that goes for you, too, Benjamin, Beny thought, exhaling the hydro smoke from his nostrils.

* * * * *

"Motherfucking eight ball, I say!" Charles screamed as he aimed his pool stick and struck the eight ball into the right pocket. "Game over!" he exclaimed in exhilaration.

He was playing five dollars a game against a redneck soldier from Tennessee named Justin, who was a big man himself. They were both intoxicated and were very good at pool.

Earl stayed in the background and held a flirtatious conversation with the pretty Arab girl who turned out to be eighteen years old and had an Arabic name he couldn't pronounce. All she did was laugh, and she only knew one English word: American.

"So, what's good with you giving me some of that mouth of yours?" Earl asked sluggishly from the Wild Turkey whiskey.

All she did was laugh at Earl's lustful attempts.

This bitch act like she has a bomb in her ass, with all this damn laughing, Earl thought.

"Who the fuck you calling a boy?" Charles yelled at Justin.

"What do you prefer me to call you . . . a nigger boy or just dumb boy?" Justin exclaimed, enticing Charles.

Damn! Here it goes! Earl thought as he turned around in the bar stool to see Charles walk up on Justin.

"What, nigger boy? Take your best shot!" Justin said, slurring his words.

Not being one to talk when it was time to brawl, Earl walked toward both drunks and said, "Yo! What's up with the disrespect?" which caused Justin to turn around into a two-piece combo that sent him flying across the pool table.

"Holy mother!" Justin's homeboy Brandon exclaimed, charging Earl with a pool stick in his hands.

But before Brandon had made his way over to Earl, he came to his senses, dropped the stick, and exited the bar altogether.

"Stupid American! Stupid American!" the Arab girl screamed while dialing the police.

"Let's go! They're calling the police!" Earl said, running out of the bar with Charles on his heels.

The bitch knew two words, not one, Earl thought as he and Charles ran away from the bar.

When Justin awoke, he was surrounded by the Iraqi police, who had no intentions of arresting him. The people that the pretty Arab woman had called were not the police. They were ISIL, and they had them a fresh American hostage who would be perfect for what they had in store for the US soldiers. One of the Arabs struck Justin in his chin with the butt end of his AK-47 rifle and knocked him back unconscious.

* * * * *

"Umm . . . umm!" her moans were muffled by the socks stuffed in her mouth as Benjamin entered her from behind.

Damn, this dick is good! she thought as she felt his dick in her stomach.

He had her ass up and face down into the sofa in his office.

"Damn, this pussy is good, baby!" Benjamin exclaimed breathlessly.

"Umm! Umm! Umm!" They were both covered in sweat and were hoping that no sudden visitors showed up. No one would be in the studio today because everyone was preparing to be at Club Crucial in Atlanta to see Bossie live in concert. Any other time than now the both of them would be expeditious in pleasing each other. But today, Benjamin wanted to explore her and give her young pussy more than what she came for.

"Who pussy?" Benjamin asked her.

Smack!

"Who pussy, I said!"

"Yours, baby! Yours!" she yelled to Benjamin.

"Ah shit!" she screamed ecstatically as she climaxed.

Benjamin could see his handprints on her red flesh and her juices covering his dick. Her load was so thick that it looked like milk on his dick. The sight of her load caused him to explode inside of her young pussy.

"Ahh, shit!" Benjamin exclaimed, collapsing on top of his young, barely legal gorgeous bitch, who couldn't get enough of him.

Damn, shawty! Pussy too good! Benjamin thought, kissing her on the back of her neck.

NINE

C had and his homie Romel, who was eighteen years old and a notorious gun man in College Park, were sitting in the black Explorer scoping out T-Zoe and Maurice's trap. Losing clientele from the weak substance of cocaine, Chad was curious to learn the distinctiveness between their product and that of T-Zoe's, who Chad knew had to be associated with the same connect. They were watching T-Zoe's trap and waiting for a nigga named Trouble to return from visiting and loading up on more product to put out near Chad's turf. Chad was grateful for Romel, who had been down with him since they were fifteen years old. Romel had a very swarthy complexion and stood five eight and weighed 165 pounds.

"I still say we just rush the trap, shawty!" Romel said, preferring to home-invade the trap instead of sticking up their pusher.

"Naw! Them niggas got niggas on deck; it's only the two of us, shawty!" Chad retorted.

Chad knew that he could easily just run in the trap and stick up T-Zoe and Maurice. But he had other plans for his enemies.

The game is persuasive, and what always looks sweet isn't sweet, Chad thought prudently.

"Check 'em out, shawty!" Romel exclaimed, watching Trouble walk downstairs.

"Let's ride, nigga!" Romel said, pulling back the slide to this Glock .21 and chambering a round. He then pulled the black ski mask over his face.

"Let's go!" Chad said, pulling a mask over his face as he put the Explorer into drive.

Chad drove up to the driver's side of Trouble's conspicuous blue Mercury with 28-inch rims. When Trouble heard the door open and the brakes stop abruptly, he instinctively tried reaching for his Glock .17, but he was too slow as the bullets hit him in his back.

Boom! Boom!

"Awwww!"

"Shut up, nigga, and give us that shit in ya pants!" Romel screamed.

"Aww shit, man!" Trouble screamed out in pain as Romel turned him on his back and reached into his pants to grab a crumpled paper bag.

"Thank you, nigga!" Romel said, squeezing the trigger three more times into Trouble's head, ending his life.

It was rare to hear shots in College Park well beyond midnight. When T-Zoe heard the screeching tires followed by the shots, it prompted him to look outside to check the scenery. When he saw the small crowd of crackheads gathering near Trouble's car, he quickly ran downstairs.

When T-Zoe arrived, he found Trouble lying on the ground in a pool of blood . . . lifeless.

"Who did it, Pam?" T-Zoe asked, knowing that crackheads see everything.

"Two niggas, one was driving. But the one who killed Trouble, it . . . it . . . it . . . !"

Smack!

"Bitch! Spit it out!" T-Zoe yelled as he slapped Pam onto the ground, where she landed on top of Trouble's body. "Bitch! I said talk!" T-Zoe yelled in rage, pulling his Glock .21 from his waist and aiming it at Pam's head.

The other crackheads quickly left, not wanting to see the end results.

"It was Romel," Pam exclaimed tremulously and timorously.

Boom! Boom! Boom!

T-Zoe pulled the trigger repeatedly, taking Pam's life for logical reasons.

If she gave up Romel, she'll go on 3rd and give me up as well, T-Zoe thought as he ran to close the trap. He then headed over to another low-key spot in Jonesboro.

Maurice was at the Boosie concert at Club Crucial and would be upset for losing Trouble.

Romel . . . I been wanting you, my nigga, T-Zoe thought as he accelerated on the interstate in his candy-red BMW.

* * * * *

Club Crucial in Atlanta was full beyond its capacity, and the women to men ratio was three to one that night. On stage, exiting the exhilarating crowd and serenading to their lyrics, were Antron and Lil' Boosie, who were performing their new hit "Straight Money."

Getting front row action were Shaquana and Champagne, who had in common their man's declination of coming to the club with them.

"Girl, that nigga Antron is the truth!" Shaquana yelled to Champagne, who was bouncing to his lyrics as well.

"Hell yeah! I see how he watching your ass, too," Champagne said.

"Whatever, bitch!" Shaquana exclaimed, taking a sip from her cup of peach CÎROC.

I see him too, but neither my concern nor focus is with him, Shaquana thought.

"Damn, girl! I got to pee. Walk with me to the restroom," Champagne asked, not wanting to go by herself.

"Okay, girl," Shaquana agreed.

Together, they walked through the crowd in their twin scintillating scarlet David Koma dresses and Brian Atwood pumps, slapping away touchy hands that felt on their curvaceous asses.

"Damn, lil' momma, let a nigga get a sample!" an elegant red-skinned man said as he stepped in front of Shaquana.

"Um, excuse you! Can you please get out of my way!" Shaquana screamed at the elegant man over the crunk crowd serenading to Boosie's "Wipe Me Down" hit.

Champagne, who was behind the dude and the one who had set up the paths of Maurice and Shaquana to cross, stayed in the background. She was tired of hearing how poor of a fuck Donavon was in bed.

Bitch! This the chance to get you some real dick, and I know Maurice got dick for days, Champagne thought, for they were involved sexually before she and Chad were serious.

"Damn, ma. To be real with you, if I get out your way, I may be passing up a once-in-a-lifetime opportunity!" Maurice shouted over the music.

Nigga, please! You better go somewhere with that bubblegum ass game, Shaquana wanted to say, but wasn't sure of what type of reaction she would get being rude to a stranger in the middle of Murderville.

"Well, sometimes that's for the good. Every opportunity is not promised good results."

I got her ass, Maurice thought as he retrospected on the wisdom an old man named Guru gave him: *To have a woman respond back in any form of rebuttal is to have her attention. And if you have her attention, then you have her.*

It was something that Maurice would never forget!

"So, you wanna play hardball, huh?"

"Boy, who are you?" Shaquana asked with a smile, no longer wanting to uphold her mean girl act.

"My name is Maurice. Nice meeting you. Um, what is your name?" he asked, outstretching his hand to shake Shaquana's.

When she took his hand, she saw all of the diamond and gold rings shining on his fingers and the costly bracelet and Rolex.

"Shaquana," she answered, looking at Champagne behind Maurice.

When he saw Shaquana looking over his shoulder, he turned around to stare into Champagne's eyes. Together they exchanged eye winks.

"Is she with you?" Maurice asked Champagne.

"Yes, she is. Excuse me, I'll let ya'll talk. The restroom is right here," she said, dismissing herself before Shaquana could protest.

I know this ho didn't just leave me with this fine-ass nigga! Shaquana thought.

"So, can I invite you to dinner tomorrow but VIP tonight? You and your friend are welcome," Maurice asked as he came in closer to Shaquana, who immediately smelled his excessive use of Polo cologne.

"Damn, he smells good . . . looks good. And Donavon refused to come have a nice time with me. I might as well get my worth of this concert!" she said.

Having a woman in contemplation is a winner . . . and the signs to unfulfilled contentment in their lives, Maurice thought in retrospection of old man Guru's wise saying.

"Damn! Ya'll still talking . . . !"

"Champagne, shut up! How would you like to go to VIP with Maurice?"

"Shit. Why are we still standing here? Let's go!" Champagne responded.

"Okay, Maurice. We could go!" Shaquana said, with a smile on her face.

"How did you get here?" Maurice asked.

"Huh?" Shaquana exclaimed in bewilderment. *What the fuck does VIP have to do with how I came here?* she thought.

"You looking like I asked you what color panties you have on!" he said.

"Then what's the importance of knowing what car I drove here?"

"Did you ever hear of Sky Lounge?"

"Sky Lounge? Hell yeah we heard of it, and we don't have no Sky Lounge money!" Shaquana said.

"Whoever said that money was a problem?" Maurice retorted.

"Okay, let's go!" Champagne and Shaquana exclaimed in unison as they looked over at each other.

T EN

Sky Lounge was a popular club in Atlanta where the scenery of the club took place on the rooftop of a skyscraper. When Maurice arrived with the two gorgeous women on both sides of him, holding onto his arms, he felt like the man in the spotlight.

"This place is beautiful!" Shaquana screamed out to Maurice over the serenading club, shouting out the lyrics to Drake's new hit "Summer Sixteen."

"Yeah . . . and VIP is over there!" Maurice yelled back, steering both women toward the exquisite and breathtaking VIP section that was under a massive neon light. Maurice pulled out a fat wad of cash from his True Religion jeans and paid $900 for everyone's entrance.

Damn, I know what he does for a living, Shaquana thought as they were led to a back corner section close to the edge of the building.

"Good to know that no one is afraid of heights," Maurice said.

"If I was, I wouldn't tell you!" Shaquana yelled.

"Yeah, right!" Champagne said as she started grooving to the Beyoncé song "Drunk in Love." She then exclaimed, "Girl, that's my shit!"

"I'll be right back. What do you ladies want to drink on?"

"Bacardi 151!" both girls replied.

"Okay then . . . I'll be back," Maurice announced.

"Girl, you gotta get that nigga's number and . . ."

"Cham . . . !"

"Girl, I don't want to hear it. Donovan stood you up, and Chad stood me up. If he wasn't after you, then I'd be all in his grill. Bitch, get the nigga number, and maybe we could look back out for him bringing us to this 'nigga-can't-afford' club!"

"Bitch, you is stupid!" Shaquana exclaimed as she broke down laughing hysterically at Champagne's risibility.

"Naw, for real, Shaquana. The nigga looks like Drake. At least do it for your best friend!" Champagne said sincerely.

Shaquana knew that Champagne loved her beyond measure and wanted to see her happy. There wasn't nothing that she kept back from Champagne. And she knew without a doubt that her true friend was the same way. It was Champagne who she felt comfortable to tell all her worries and saddest moments. Champagne knew more than what her mom was supposed to know—and that she was not happy with Donavon.

"Okay, girl. I will get his number!" Shaquana said as soon as Maurice had made it back. In his hands were two cups of Bacardi, which he passed over to each girl.

"What! Don't you drink?" Shaquana asked when she didn't see a cup in Maurice's hand.

"If you don't mind, I'll sip with you," he responded.

What the fuck is he on? Shaquana thought, wondering what kind of dude took a stranger out and drank from her glass.

"Is it worse than kissing?" Maurice asked, reading her mind. But when she looked at his lips, her mood fluctuated.

That nigga do got some sexy lips. Cheer up, girl! Shaquana told herself.

"It's okay. Only if you tell me that I'm the first girl you've met in one night and drank out of her cup!" Shaquana asked.

"I've done a lot of things more dirty than that on the first night with a girl, and it all counted as fun!" Maurice responded.

"So nasty! You got that one!" Shaquana joked.

"You asked for it!" Champagne said as she downed her drink.

"Refill please," Champagne said as she held out her cup for Maurice to refill from the bottle tucked between his armpits. Shaquana did the same.

"Now you can drink, and then pass it to me!" Shaquana said.

Neither woman tasted the distinctive taste of Molly in their drinks. Rihanna's song came on, and both friends got their groove on with Maurice in VIP, going cup for cup and having a splendid time.

"Bitch better have my money!" Shaquana and Champagne screamed, serenading to the Rihanna lyrics.

* * * * *

T-Zoe was shacked up with his youngest and most gorgeous sidekick. They were only established as fucking friends who enjoyed the pleasure that each gave the other. She was sixteen years old, of Haitian descent, and had a scintillating body. Her oldest sister, Bay-Bay, was at work, and she had no clue that her sister Cindy had a man in her apartment other than Daquan, who Bay-Bay liked as a decent brother-in-law. Despite how ill Bay-Bay would be if she ever discovered how much of a slut her baby sister was, Cindy loved money and sex. And that was what Bay-Bay wasn't giving her. Cindy and T-Zoe had been fucking for hours and had sexed each other into exhaustion. Cuddled up in his arms while rubbing on his stomach, Cindy immersed below the covers and placed T-Zoe's dick in her mouth, slowly giving him oral sex and arousing his manhood again.

"Damn, ma!" T-Zoe said, feeling as if he was about to explode. "Damn, bitch. You got a superb head game," he shouted as he exploded inside Cindy's mouth, where she swallowed every bit of his load.

"Umm!" she moaned out loud.

"Yes, baby. Damn!" T-Zoe exclaimed in ecstasy as Cindy continued to arouse him again.

When she had him standing tall again, she climbed on top of him and slowly slid down his length.

"Ahhh!" Cindy moaned as she slowly rode him, feeling him deep inside her womb.

The way she felt, she wanted it to last forever. It was bliss that she could name it . . . and pure ecstasy is what it was.

Despite her age, Cindy was grown in her mind, but she only loved one person in her life: Daquan.

* * * * *

Both women were inebriated and feeling themselves like never before, constantly laughing and more than twice having to be rescued after falling to the ground. The Molly inside the Bacardi bottle and the E pills had them on cloud ecstasy. On the dance floor, Maurice had made his move against Shaquana by licking her behind her ear while caressing her soft, smooth ass. His every touch sent a wave of electricity through her body. The way she was feeling while grooving with him was ineffable. And both of them couldn't resist their affection for each other, both lost in their erogenous zones for each other. It didn't take much for Maurice to get Champagne in the picture. Something that was extemporaneous but worked out fine, because he now had two beautiful women walking through the door of his hotel suite. As soon as the door closed, Maurice wasted no time leading both women to the bedroom. They both were giggling like teenagers and were being naughty just because.

Maurice stepped out of the room to go order more liquor and left the two inebriated friends alone.

"Girl, this nigga done brought us to a nice-ass hotel."

"What he think . . . he gonna get some pussy? I can't even lie, girl. The way his hands felt on my booty made me wet," Shaquana exclaimed laggardly.

"Girl, so let him beat your back in shit!" Champagne said in the same manner encouragingly.

"Is you crazy, girl? I don't know him."

"That's more thrill to the curiosity if you ask me," Champagne said, lying back on the bed and taking her pumps off.

"What's wrong with you doing it with him then?" Shaquana stood up and asked Champagne after almost falling, at which both girls burst into laughter.

"Girl, that ain't funny!" Shaquana said, sitting back down on the bed.

"Well, sit your clumsy ass down!" Champagne retorted.

"And to answer your crazy-ass question, do you think he brought both of us here to fuck one?" Champagne asked.

"Girl, he thinks he slick, huh?"

"No, girl. He wants to have fun, and we shouldn't have no problem in having fun too," Champagne explained.

Damn! She telling me to fuck this stranger, Shaquana thought. *Maybe it would be fun!*

"You go first!"

"No. We go together," Champagne answered.

"A threesome, girl?"

"Something wrong with that, sexy?" Maurice said as he came into the room with another bottle of Bacardi 151 in his hand, with just his plaid Polo briefs on.

Oh my God! This nigga is fine as hell. He looks just like Drake, she thought as he came closer to her and stood behind her legs.

"So, you down? Or will you shut me down and leave me and Champagne to ourselves? A little help from you would capture this night as a splendid memory," Maurice said as he rubbed Shaquana's smooth face.

"Yes!" Shaquana said as she stuck her tongue out and licked Maurice's thumb seductively. This time, she made the first move.

Maurice leaned down and met her sexy lips. When he parted her lips with his tongue, he went inside her mouth, and Shaquana let out a moan: "Ummm!"

As he kissed her passionately and slowly, Champagne undressed herself down to nothing and began massaging her throbbing clitoris while looking at Maurice.

It's getting hot in here, Shaquana thought, drowning in his kisses.

Maurice was enthralled at seeing Champagne's plump shaved pussy, which aroused him to an extraordinary erection, no doubt caused by the Viagra that he took thirty minutes before. When he sat up, Shaquana gasped for breath upon catching a view of his full erection that shot through the slot of his briefs.

Damn, this nigga is packing. I can't believe I'm doing this, Shaquana thought as he took off his briefs and climbed into bed. He crawled in between Champagne's legs, where he started gently sucking and licking on her clitoris.

"Yes, eat this pussy!" Champagne moaned, and she spread her legs wider.

Shaquana wasted no time coming out of her dress, pumps, and black lingerie. Her pussy was excessively wet and her clitoris throbbing. *He wasn't Jarvis, but he was far away from Donavon,* Shaquana thought as she climbed on the bed with Champagne and Maurice.

He immediately began to suck on Shaquana's erect nipples, causing her to moan out to him. The titillation was sweet and electrifying as he caressed her breasts and sucked on her nipples.

"Ma, ride my face and spurt that good shit on me," Maurice demanded of Shaquana.

Being ingenuous, she wasted no time and satisfied Maurice, who taught her every step of the way what a threesome rally was while he ate her pussy good. She gyrated her hips, cumming on his face twice while Champagne rode his dick in the reverse cowgirl position.

Damn, this nigga tongue game is superb, Shaquana thought as she climaxed.

The trio pleased each other in different positions until dawn came, enjoying multiple electrifying orgasms. Shaquana had to give it to Maurice. He proved to be a replacement for the unfulfilled necessity in her sex life. But she couldn't leave her man for another man who had her homegirl as well. That's one thing that she could say good about Donavon, and it felt good to know that fact.

The trio lay in bed, Shaquana being the only one not asleep. Still feeling the intoxication from the Bacardi and drugs, unbeknownst to her, she wanted to feel Maurice inside her one more time before they departed and ended their amazing one-night fling. Immersing discreetly beneath the covers, she took Maurice into her mouth, causing him to wake and lift up the covers.

"Damn ma . . . !"

"Shhhh . . . Don't wake her," Shaquana said as she emerged from the bed and walked toward the bedroom door. She turned around partially nude and looked into Maurice's adoring eyes. He took in the sight of her curves and got hard as a rock again.

"Damn!" he sighed in passion and lust.

Without speaking, Shaquana gestured with her index finger and told Maurice to follow her. He looked at Champagne, who was asleep, and quietly emerged from the bed to follow Shaquana into the bathroom. There, they took a warm shower together and pleased each other again.

When Champagne heard the moans coming from the shower over Kelly Rowland's "Motivation" emanating from her iPhone, she smiled and cuddled up inside the comfortable covers.

I'm proud of you, daughter. Yes, I am, Champagne thought. *Soon, Donavon will be out of the picture because no woman stays away from good dick*, she kept thinking, obviously being able to speak vicariously from experience.

Feeling him deep inside her womb as the warm water cascaded down her back was most definitely a fulfillment of what she was missing in her life. Shaquana held onto the back of his neck, with her head in his chest as he thrust in and out of her from behind, simultaneously caressing her erect nipples. She wanted it to last forever, since she had never been fucked in such a manner. She'd never had an organism from a man's penetration alone. And it felt great.

"Umm! Umm! Uh! Uhh!" she moaned out as he went deeper, hitting her G-spot with every stroke.

"Damn, shawty! This pussy is too good and tight!" Maurice whispered in her ear breathlessly.

"Yes! Yes! Uhhh! I'm cumming, Maurice!" Shaquana moaned as her body trembled from her electrifying orgasm. "Oh shit! Maurice!"

"This dick champion, shawty!" Maurice said as he continued to pound her pussy in the midst of her climaxing. When he felt his dick being gripped by her walls, he lost control and came to a powerful load himself.

"Ahh, shit!" he groaned out as he pulled out of her pussy and shot his load on her ass and back.

Learning the game from her mother, Shaquana immediately urinated in an effort to push out the semen that didn't have time to follow the rest out of her womb.

I damn sho' don't need any kids right now, especially from no stranger. But the dick is good, she thought while peeing down the drain. When she was done, she allowed Maurice to assist her in washing her body, whereas she then returned the favor.

This is what Donavon is supposed to be doing. How could a stranger do it so confidently and better? Shaquana wanted to know.

ELEVEN

"You know what, Jarvis, we could go on and on about your stubbornness, as long as we understand that change would immediately come," Benjamin said to a pugnacious Jarvis.

"Your problem, Benjamin, is that you only care about your damn self. Nigga, I had to lie to Renae about your . . ."

"Nigga, you have no right to come at me sideways!" Benjamin yelled as he jumped out of his seat, ready to pounce on Jarvis, who was sitting on the sofa in front of his desk.

"Nigga, what, you ready to put your hands on me? Let's talk about being too potent," Jarvis said, slowly standing in case he had to defend himself.

I be damned I let this nigga put his hands on me. I don't care how much game he gave me, Jarvis thought

"Naw, nigga. If I have to put my hands on you, then it means that I don't love you, nigga. So before I do that, I'ma give you time to get your act together."

"Benjamin, you're the one bent out of shape. I can't be your assistant or right-hand man if you overriding my authority on every corner. And especially about one of your hos, nigga!" Jarvis expressed himself, almost foaming at the mouth.

"And what can you do about your boss over your head, huh?" Benjamin asked, folding his arms across his chest while mugging Jarvis, who became speechless. "Yeah, you're getting the picture now, huh? Because there ain't shit you can do about it, just like a million other motherfuckers in your position," Benjamin said veraciously from a logical perspective.

He is right, but this nigga will not try me like a buster, Jarvis thought.

"Man! Straight up, if you giving me the room to make a decision, then why override me?"

"Because what Benjamin says . . . goes, damn it!" Benjamin exploded, pounding his fist on the desk in a violent rage that sent papers flying everywhere. "You know what, Jarvis?" Benjamin continued, stepping in his face.

"Put your hands on me, and I will show you what you've created!" Jarvis threatened.

"Get the fuck outta my face, before I kill you!" Benjamin barked, pointing toward the door.

This nigga just threatened to take my life, Jarvis thought.

"Damn, Ben . . . them words mean too much!"

"And I mean every word of it, by all means, nigga. Now beat your feet like you've been doing and don't return," Benjamin exclaimed.

"Nigga, you can't do this shit without me!" Jarvis screamed out in rage.

"Nigga, I said go!" Benjamin said between clenched teeth with fire in his eyes.

"So this is the result of consultation?" Jarvis asked.

"It's the best advice that I've been giving you since carrying your ass at fifteen, and I hope you take heed to do what's right!" Benjamin said coldly.

With nothing else to say, Jarvis turned on his heels and left the studio altogether. The only thing that was on his mind as he walked toward his black-on-black Benz truck was making Benjamin live up to his words.

"No man would ever live telling me that they would kill me," Jarvis said vindictively as he left the premises. *I'ma make that nigga prove me wrong*, he thought, silently crying.

* * * * *

Sitting at his desk and cracking his knuckles with a menacing look on his face, Benjamin was up to his neck with putting up with Jarvis's inferiority complex. He didn't care how much their bond was worth. He was tired of the problems that came along with it.

My business is my business, and what and how I did it was Benjamin. He talking about he had to lie to my wife about me. Nigga . . . get off that ho shit acting like he wearing panties, Benjamin thought. While looking at his phone in contemplation on dialing out, he made his mind up, picked up the receiver, and called Renae, who picked up on the second ring.

"Hello!" Renae answered, enraptured.

"What's up, baby?" Benjamin asked, leaning back in his comfortable chair, kicking his feet up onto the desk, and crossing his ankles. To hear her voice was always music to his ears.

"Nothing, baby. I'm just stepping inside the house. Getting back from shopping. Are you okay? You sound like something is wrong, baby." Renae said, knowing her husband.

"It's okay. I'm just thinking about this new contract deal in Philly," Benjamin lied.

"Well, don't let it beat you, baby," Renae retorted.

"I love you, Renae," he said, unconsciously aware of why he felt the need to remind her. And he sensed that Renae felt the same, judging by her split second of silence.

"Baby, are you in trouble? I love you too, but you make it seem like it's the last I love you . . ."

"Baby, stop what you are doing and come make love to me in this comfortable chair I'm sitting in," Benjamin demanded.

"Ben!"

"Renae!" Benjamin mocked her.

"Are you serious?" she asked.

"You find out!" Benjamin said, hanging up the phone.

If there was anyone that he could count on, it was his down-to-earth wife. Without a doubt, he knew that she'd be coming through the door soon. So he undressed himself and waited for his queen.

Nigga, when you have it like me, then you can question my decisions. A real player never wears his feelings on his sleeves, Benjamin thought to himself to assuage the anguish that had all of a sudden overtaken him as he waited for his wife to show.

He rubbed his face with both hands in hopes of wiping away his stress.

* * * * *

"Damn, nigga. So that nigga Romel stunting like that, huh?" Maurice asked T-Zoe, who had just given him the news of Trouble's robbery and death. As he expected, Maurice was upset and ready to go after Chad.

That's why I fucked that nigga bitch last night. Only if the nigga knew. Shit, I'll let him know her worth when I catch his ass, Maurice thought as he walked back and forth in the living room of their trap.

"So tell me this, shawty. What we going to do?" Maurice asked T-Zoe, stopping in front of him and sitting on the sofa smoking a dro blunt, exhaling the smoke.

"I say we lay low and continue to get this money. We have lil' niggas to squeeze our triggers now, let's remember."

"Wrong answer, T-Zoe. I say we close shop and bring it to them niggas head-on. Fuck all this peace shit! Before the money, we were laying these niggas down, and that's what we need to continue to do. Because obviously, these niggas think the 3rd is pussy," Maurice exclaimed, taking notice that T-Zoe was getting so relaxed in the lavishness that he wasn't even himself anymore.

On any other day before they started seeing real cash coming from the dope game, T-Zoe would have attended the Boosie concert with him and had a chance to fuck Champagne. But letting money blow his mind, he would never discover that he'd missed his golden chance to fuck Ms. Champagne, a bitch who he'd had twice on two different occasions.

"Man, let's lay low and get this money, shawty. We'll have plenty time to make these niggas pay," T-Zoe said.

"You could sit here and wait for these niggas to run down on you. I know where to find these niggas myself," Maurice said, storming out the door in search of his enemies.

* * * * *

Tameka had just made it home from her second job, and she was over-exhausted.

I can't believe these motherfuckers still don't have new employees to fill in the empty positions, she thought as she tore open her mail.

"Bill, bill, bills!" she said as she looked at her preposterous light bill.

"What the fuck! Eight hundred dollars for motherfucking using the lights?" Tameka screamed in disbelief.

Knock! Knock! Knock!

Who the hell is knocking on my door, Tameka wanted to know, finding it strange because no one knew where she lived, being that she kept a low profile. As she walked toward the door, she thought of one individual who could possibly be at the door and she smiled—elated at being able to see him again.

I knew that he would come back, Tameka thought as she carelessly opened the door without first looking out the peephole.

However, when she saw who the person was, her smile quickly vanished, and her elation was replaced with fear from the look in his eyes.

What the fuck is he doing here? she wondered.

"Jarvis, what are you do—"

Before Tameka could get the word out of her mouth, Jarvis delivered a powerful blow to her jaw, knocking her completely out. Satisfied, he stepped over her unconscious body and closed the door to her apartment. He dragged her by her hair across the carpet and into her bedroom, where he stripped her of all her clothes.

"Bitch! You think that you could get away from me, huh?" Jarvis exclaimed as he entered her forcefully. Tameka awoke in pain as he entered her from behind. She just lay there nonresistant, letting him have his way with her. She knew that fighting back would only make him mad. And the last thing she wanted was to entice him and add more fuel to the flames.

He found me. I can't believe this! Tameka thought as tears fell from her eyes, and as her pain turned into pleasure. To make him happy, she threw her pussy back into his strokes.

"Umm, Jarvis!" Tameka moaned out, giving him what he wanted—and what he would die for, even if it took killing her so that she wouldn't be with another. She was ready to do it.

Save me now, Benjamin. Save me from this monster! Tameka prayed to the man she needed at the moment—and forever—but was far from her rescue.

She realized that playing hard to get had resulted in her nightmare being able to hurt her again.

He found me, but how? she thought, with tears cascading down her face.

T WELVE

When Donavon got the phone call, he was elated and felt like a million-dollar man. Berlinda was back in Atlanta from LA, where he was filming a movie, playing a deceiving transgendered man who tricks a big-time pimp in New York. He was good at it, since he did it well in real life with no problem. The plus points for Berlinda came when those who did find out the truth wanted to continue on with the relationship. Donavon was one of the few men who Berlinda had wrapped around his fingers, but he was tired of waiting for Donavon to get rid of Shaquana.

"Damn! It's been a long three weeks since I seen my baby," Donavon exclaimed as he strutted from Gary's Law Firm, where he was a paralegal, to his car parked across the street.

Shit, I promised Shaquana that I was going out with her tonight, to make up for not going to the Boosie concert, Donavon remembered as he merged into traffic.

He turned up the volume on the radio and let music from Kem emanate throughout the Lexus 6 x 9 speakers.

"Share me life!" Donavon exclaimed joyfully, serenading to Kem's hit.

Fuck that, I'll tell Shaquana that I have to work late tonight, Donavon thought, satisfied with how he would dodge her tonight. There was nothing more in the world that he wanted in his life than what was making him happy, his relationship with Berlinda.

"Damn, I love that bitch!" Donavon said, speaking of Berlinda.

* * * * *

"Daquan, come help me with these potatoes!" Renae yelled as she walked into the den, where he was playing NBA 2016 on his Xbox 360. "And for the umpteenth time, negro, stop scratching your damn balls! You've been doing that shit all day. Maybe you need to go bathe," Renae said to him.

"Alright, Mom. I'm coming. Let me finish this stage first"

"Shaquana," Renae yelled upstairs.

"Yes, Mom!"

"Come help me in this kitchen."

"Mom, I'm getting ready to leave. Why can't Daquan help?"

I know this heifer didn't. These kids think they're going to sit on their asses while I do all the work, Renae thought as she walked back into the kitchen. On her way back, she observed Daquan once again scratching his nuts.

"Daquan, c'mere . . . and I mean now!" Renae called for him when a troubling prospect came to mind.

"Yes, Mom!" Daquan said as he stood up and walked toward her, unconsciously aware that he was scratching again. "Yes, Mom!" he continued as he halted in front of her.

"Are you having sex, Daquan?" she asked, already knowing that her son was fucking—and probably even earlier than she had ever expected.

At just nine years old, Daquan was a precocious child. Something that Renae saw for the good or bad beforehand. But the question from his mom caught him off guard and left him speechless.

"So, you're not going to answer me, boy!" Renae exclaimed, crossing her arms across her chest and giving him one of her menacing motherly looks.

"Mom. What is sex?"

"Boy, don't play with me. Sex is what got you here!" Renae said, slapping him on the back of his head, like his dad would do.

"Yes, Mom. I get my groove on," Daquan answered abashedly, with his head down.

"With how many?" Renae quickly retorted.

"Just one, Mom."

"When was the last time?"

"Two weeks ago, Mom" Daquan answered, feeling uncomfortable with having the conversation with his mother.

"Did ya'll use protection?" she asked.

Getting no direct response from Daquan was concisely enough to answer her question.

"Pull your pants and drawers down to your ankles, Daquan!"

"What!" Daquan exclaimed in shock.

"Boy, don't what me! Now do as I say. I'm your momma, and I brought you into this world. I'm the reason you have a dick," Renae said.

"I can't believe this. It has to be the most embarrassing thing to do in life," Daquan said.

"Daquan Coleman Clark, if I have to tell you again, mister, to pull down your pants, I know something!" Renae exclaimed.

Daquan knew that when his mom called out his entire name, that she was ready to explode.

"If it's that serious, Mom, I guess," Daquan said, pouting as he unbuckled his skinny jeans and let them fall to the ground.

Renae grabbed a hold of Daquan's penis and squeezed the head softly.

"Aww, Mom!" he cried out in pain.

"Son, it is serious. Boy, your dick is swollen and got pus discharging. Lord, this boy has gonorrhea!" Renae exclaimed, putting her hands on her forehead in frustration.

"Shaquana, get your ass down here now!" Renae screamed.

"Yes, Mom," she hastened downstairs, simultaneously responding.

"Did I hear that someone has gonorrhea?" Shaquana asked while watching her brother re-fasten his skinny jeans.

"Yeah, your damn brother done let some girl give it to him, and I hope that he knows what it means, if she's the only girl he's been so-called fucking," Renae exclaimed mordantly, with her hands on her hips.

"It means she's having sex elsewhere, little brother."

The reality hit Daquan hard. He loved Cindy and was only having sex with her, when he could have been sexing plenty of women his age and beyond.

I can't believe this bitch! he thought, heartbroken—which was evident to his mom and sister by the inevitable tears cascading down his face.

"Son, you're going to be alright. It's nothing that you can't get rid of. After this, you just got to start using protection," Renae said, hugging her son in a motherly embrace.

"Shaquana . . . me and your brother are going to the doctor. Please watch them turkey necks and greens and the cornbread in the oven until I get back," Renae ordered.

Shaquana knew that to protest wouldn't be wise and that her family came first before her pleasure.

"Okay, Mom. I'll be here when you get back," she responded. She knew she had crossed the line by indulging in unprotected sex with Maurice.

I just pray that he has a clean dick. It will never happen again. The only one who was fucking me without protection was Donavon, and it will stay like that, Shaquana thought as she started chopping the potatoes for her mom's delicious potato salad.

* * * * *

Haitian Beny and his two bodyguards had pulled up to Pleasures no later than expected. They all stepped out of the black Chevy Tahoe truck and walked through the back door of the club, where the trio was escorted to an opulent office to await Benjamin.

"He'll be with ya'll soon. Can I be of any help with any accommodations?" exclaimed Benjamin's bouncer, Big Dee, who stood six seven, with a swarthy complexion.

"Just a bottle of Remy, shawty," Beny said, handing over two duffel bags containing a half million dollars in hundred dollar bills to get counted for their next re-up.

"Okay," Big Dee said, leaving the trio alone.

In another room, Benjamin watched the trio from a camera monitor as Big Dee walked inside and dumped the money on a long cherry-wood conference table.

"Looks like it's here . . . every dime of it!" Big Dee said.

"Has anybody seen Majik?" Benjamin asked, concerned that she had not shown up all week as well as her negligence in returning any of his calls.

"Naw, Ben, haven't seen Ms. Majik. I thought maybe she was sick," Big Dee answered.

"Tell DJ Spine to call Majik and see if she's coming in," Benjamin demanded as he left the room with the same duffel bags filled with fifteen kilos of raw cocaine. He then walked into his office where Haitian Beny and his two men awaited him.

"How are we doing, Beny?" Benjamin asked as he stepped into the office. He greeted Beny with a business-like handshake and dropped the bags by his feet.

"Slowly progressing . . . with the help of a real friend," Beny retorted, taking his seat again.

Just as Benjamin took his seat, the door opened. Big Dee stuck his head in and tossed a bottle of Remy Martin inside to Beny, with three plastic cups.

"Thanks, shawty," Beny said as he immediately poured his men a cup of Remy with no ice.

"You're welcome . . . and no answer, Ben. I'll be in the club if you need me."

Shit, where the fuck is she? Benjamin thought as he checked the time on his Rolex and saw that it was 2:00 a.m. *Shit is crazy!*

He was eager to see her to break the ice of his feelings for her. There were a lot of strippers that needed a new assistant boss, and Benjamin thought that Majik would fit the criterion.

"Thank you, Big Dee," Benjamin said. He then waited until his bodyguard was gone before he continued. "Okay, Beny. That's fifteen bricks. Anything else you need . . . just hit me up," he said with his hands clamped together.

"I need a partner, Benjamin, who I know would have my back to the door . . ."

There we go again, Benjamin thought.

"We could lock down this whole East Coast together, Ben," Beny said.

"Beny, I can be inspired by your consideration on consolidating. But like I've told you, I'm . . ."

This nigga want to feed me like a fish, huh! Beny thought, with a frown on his face

"We cool, Beny . . . but like I said, to get where I'm at now, I got here by myself," Benjamin reiterated to him again, hitting his chest.

"Nice doing business with you, Benjamin, but whether you like it or not, I plan on being the man that I left by all means. This is my last time copping from you. And trust me . . . I plan to make your world a living hell!"

"Nigga! What you saying?" Benjamin said as he jumped out of his seat, feeling offended by Beny's effronteries and curveball threats.

"I meant what I said, nigga. Take it how you see it," Beny said, with Big Funk and Corey ready to pounce on Benjamin if he made the wrong move.

Their guns were drawn at their sides, and despite being one move away from his, Benjamin knew well of the statistics of prevailing against the odds.

"We'll see each other again, but not on friendly grounds," Haitian Beny said, taking a swig from the Remy bottle before walking out of the office and out of the nightclub altogether.

Without Jarvis, he was limited to muscle.

Finally feeling the effect of his mistake, he cursed himself, because he knew what was coming, but not the impact. "Fuck!" he yelled.

T HIRTEEN

D aquan couldn't get any sleep as he lay in his bed, thinking of Cindy's betrayal to him.

I can't believe this bitch, he thought, sitting up in his bed and looking at the clock on his nightstand. It was 3:00 a.m.

I'll be damned. I let this ho get away with betraying me, Daquan thought as he emerged from bed and put on an all-black outfit and skully. He quietly walked downstairs and into the den, where he walked out of the house through a side door.

It was foggy and chilly, but he had on proper clothes to defeat Mother Nature. Daquan hopped on his candy-red cruiser bike and peddled to Tittyboo's house, which was just two blocks away. Seeing the TV still on, he knew that he was still awake.

This nigga pulls all-nighters and makes it look easy, he thought as he hopped off the bicycle and went to knock on the door. Before he could knock, the door swung open, and there stood Tittyboo, with no shirt on, exposing his protruding, hefty belly, with a blunt in his mouth.

"Boy . . . Benjamin and Renae are going to kill your ass for being out this late . . . on a school night at that!" Tittyboo exclaimed, letting Daquan into the house.

"What's wrong, shawty?" Tittyboo asked, seeing the distressed look on his friend's face as he passed him the hydro blunt that was laced with Molly and a mixture of other combined drugs called flakka. Being in too much upheaval, and ingenuous, Daquan couldn't detect the distinctiveness.

"Man, that ho gave me gonorrhea, Titty!" Daquan explained, exhaling the flakka.

"Who, shawty?" Tittyboo asked in feigned surprise, for he knew that Cindy was fucking a handful of other men. He just didn't know how to bring it up to his friend without causing him the pain that he was now in.

"What do you mean who, nigga? The only bitch I'm fucking!" Daquan retorted.

"Damn, shawty!" Tittyboo exclaimed in empathy.

"Let me hold the flame (gun), shawty!" Daquan asked.

"Flame?" Tittyboo replied. "Naw, shawty. That ho ain't worth it."

"Man, I ain't about to murk the bitch. I'm just gonna scare her up a little and slap the bitch around," Daquan said.

"Alright, shawty . . . hold on," Tittyboo said, not wanting to rub Daquan wrong by continuing to protest letting him hold the gun. Daquan paced the living room back and forth impatiently, unaware of the flakka taking its effect on him.

When Tittyboo returned with the black .357 and handed it to Daquan, he saw a look in his eyes that deeply troubled him.

Damn! I hope he don't do nothing stupid, Tittyboo thought as he watched Daquan put the .357 in his front waistband.

"I'll bring it back in the morning," Daquan said as he left out the front door and hopped back on his bike.

"Be smart, homeboy," Tittyboo called out as he closed the door, regretting ever letting his true friend go out into the world a mad man with a gun.

* * * * *

Benjamin had left the club early and hopped on the interstate on his way to Atlanta. On the passenger side, he had a dozen roses and a get well card embellished with a unique art design. When he got off the interstate and shortly made it to the apartment complex, he killed the engine to his luxurious Jaguar and exited with the roses in hand. It was 4:00 a.m., and he had no intentions of leaving anytime soon. When he knocked on apartment #212, he was anxious and more elated on making the surprise visit.

"Come on, baby girl. Open the door!" he said, knocking on the door three more times.

When he heard indiscernible voices, he became puzzled. The last thing he'd ever thought to consider was her having company.

Damn, I hope I ain't invading. I'll say I'm her boss, Benjamin thought.

"Bitch, don't play with me!"

Smack!

"Aww, Jarvis!" Tameka screamed out in pain from the slap.

"What the fuck!" Benjamin exclaimed as he heard the door being unlocked.

What the fuck this ho got Jarvis in her shit for? he thought as the door swung open.

"Nigga, what the fuck do you want, huh?"

Instead of an answer, Benjamin quickly stole on Jarvis with a three-piece combination while still gripping the roses in his balled fist. The impact from his blows was only powerful enough to knock Jarvis down, who quickly but dazedly got back up to defend himself.

"Oh my God!" Tameka screamed as she watched Jarvis charge Benjamin, who side-stepped him and connected another three-piece combination that sent him flying into the living room, onto a glass table, shattering it into pieces.

Before Jarvis had time to come back to his feet, Benjamin delivered a powerful kick to his temple, knocking him completely out. When Benjamin saw that Jarvis was out cold, he rushed over to Tameka, who was crying hysterically on the hallway floor.

"Majik, baby, are you okay?" Benjamin asked as he knelt down and wrapped his arms around her.

"Please . . . just go before you make it worse. Please go!" she cried out, covering her face with a wet towel.

"Baby, who is he?" Benjamin wanted to know of the man who he thought would be the Jarvis he knew when the door first opened. But the man lying in the living room was out cold and didn't look like "his" Jarvis at all. He was five eight and too damn black to be Jarvis.

"He's my crazy-ass boyfriend," Tameka said as she removed the towel from her face, revealing her battered face. "What the fuck!" Benjamin screamed out in disbelief and hurt, now realizing why she had been absent from work.

"Do you love him?" Benjamin asked, lifting up her face by her chin, looking in her one good eye that had a single tear falling.

"No, Benjamin. I don't love him," Tameka said as she broke down.

Without saying another word, Benjamin picked her up and carried her to his car. He placed her safely in the passenger side seat. When he went into the glove compartment and retrieved his Glock .19, Tameka attempted to stop him by putting her hands on his wrist.

"He's not worth it, Ben!"

"Do you love him?" Benjamin asked again.

"No, Ben . . . but he's no . . ."

Before she could get her words out, Benjamin closed the door and walked back toward the apartment. When he stepped inside, the man was sitting up and rubbing his jaw. When he saw Benjamin with the gun in his hands, he tried shielding the shots with his hands, but to no avail.

"Bitch ass nigga!" Benjamin yelled as he pulled the trigger.

Boom! Boom! Boom! Boom! Boom!

When Tameka heard the shots, she cried out hysterically, but not because she was in pain or because she knew had just happened. She cried because she was finally free. Jarvis would never be able to hurt her again.

Boom!

Hearing the last shot, she knew that it was over and that Benjamin wanted her to be just as safe as she did.

* * * * *

When Daquan had arrived at his girlfriend Cindy's apartment, he saw that Bay-Bay's car was gone, which told him that she was still at work. But there was an unknown, conspicuous car in her parking space. As Daquan knocked on the door, he had no clue what he was there to actually do. On the third round of knocking, Cindy came to open the door.

"Daquan, what are you doing here? It's 5:00 in the morning," she said, crossing her arms and getting goose bumps from the chilly air wafting into the apartment.

"Cindy, are you cheating on me?" he asked, with a cold stare that scared her. She had never seen Daquan look at her that way before.

"No, why do you ask that silly question?"

"Whatever!" Daquan said, attempting to walk inside before being stopped at Cindy's protest.

"No, Daquan. Bay-Bay is coming home, and she wants nobody over," Cindy ordered as she held her hands out pressed against his chest to stop him from entering any further.

"Cindy, get your damn hands off me!" he yelled through clenched teeth.

Before he could give her a chance to remove her hands, he grabbed her by her throat and pinned her against the wall, pulling the gun from his waist and placing it to her head.

"No, Daquan! Please don't do this. I love you!" Cindy shouted, pleading for him to hear her cries of love.

She had no clue of the stranger that held her by the throat with a gun pressed against her head.

"Bitch! Tell me who you are fucking?" Daquan asked in an abnormal voice.

The apartment was dark, and the only light came from the TV in the room. She could see the fire in his eyes and foam coming from his mouth.

"What the fuck!"

Boom! Boom!

Startled by the voice of a figure in the darkness that came from across the room, Daquan's hallucinations made him think it was the devil. His ears rang from the loud shots as he walked toward the figure now lying on the floor.

He then saw snakes and fired the gun again.

Boom! Boom! Boom!

"Daquan! Nooooo!"

At the sound of his name, Daquan turned around and saw a female devil lashing out at him with a sword as a tongue. Scared of being hurt, he fired at the female figure's head.

Boom!

As he continued to squeeze the trigger, he realized that the gun was empty. The lady was gone. She was dead.

He ran nonstop as fast as he could, from the apartment all the way home.

When he made it home with the gun still in his hand, he became nauseous and vomited in his driveway. Daquan hurried inside the house through the same side door and crashed on the den's sofa, stuffing the murder weapon under the sofa's pillow. He had no clue that he'd just killed Cindy and T-Zoe.

As he slept, he dreamt of a pretty mermaid who he had fallen in love with and married. Her name was Cindy. But it was just a dream; something that he would wish for come morning.

F OURTEEN

Tameka had no clue where Benjamin was taking her. The entire ride was in silence. Neither one said anything to the other. Despite the silence, she knew that Benjamin was married, which meant that he was not bringing her home like she so badly wanted.

Maybe he's a widow, Tameka thought. Her curiosity had gotten the best of her, and she needed to know.

"Is she dead?" she said, breaking the silence as she continued to look forward. Benjamin looked over at Majik, hating to see what she was going through.

If anyone deserves a word of honesty, it sure is her—and any woman in her position, he thought sympathetically.

"What are you talking about?"

"You're married, Benjamin. It's not like we're about to run away together into the sunset, unless . . . ," Tameka began, before stopping short of her true feelings.

"Unless what?" he asked.

"Unless she is dead!" Tameka reiterated as she looked out the window, unable to stop the tears from falling.

"She's not dead, Majik."

"Call me Tameka. Majik died back there in that apartment!" she told him as she shielded her eye from the rays of dawn.

"Tameka, I'm sorry for what you had to go through."

"And I'm sorry that you had to come save me, Benjamin. You have no clue what my life is about, Ben. If you have a family, please go back to them."

"Why are you talking nonsense?" he asked.

"Because I know a man's heart when he's indecisive, Benjamin. Our chemistry speaks no riddles."

"Then let love be love," Benjamin said.

"How could you speak on such terms when you are married?" she asked him.

"Maybe it's not what you are perceiving, Tameka, and I could speak from my heart genuinely," Benjamin replied as he turned off the interstate and entered Jonesboro.

"There are feelings, Benjamin. I just don't want to be hurt again. You are a married man, and that's only trouble for me," she exclaimed as he turned into an expensive high-rise hotel suite. "What are we doing here, Benjamin?" Tameka asked curiously.

"Listen, please relax and trust me, Tameka, that you'll be fine. Don't get any tainted idea, as if I'm trying to take advantage of you. I'ma hold you off over here until shit clears   up.
Shower . . . and let the nurse I send care for you."

"What nurse?" she asked.

"Tameka, too many questions means doubt. Stop doubting, boo, and trust," Benjamin said, cupping her chin in his hands. Looking into her eyes, he saw a hurt woman that he longed to treat queenly in all aspects. The way she worked the pole and kept it strictly business had gotten them at this standing point, and he wanted to journey further. "You're safe and still beautiful," he said, bringing a smile to her face.

"You're lying!" she returned, trying to hide her blushing face.

As she attempted to turn away, Benjamin moved in and kissed her softly on her busted, swollen lips. He was gentle, and despite him being unable to kiss her like he wanted, it sustained as a precious moment that neither wanted to end.

"Every step of the way, I will be there," Benjamin promised, speaking concisely and meaning every word.

"Thank you, Benjamin," she said, reaching over to hug him.

Together they held each other for what seemed like an eternity.

* * * * *

When Benjamin drove into his neighborhood, he was greeted with a crime scene two blocks away from his home.

What the hell is going on now? he thought while looking at the innumerable police and detectives near Sarah's Place, an apartment complex for low-income renters.

He knew that Daquan's girlfriend lived there, but the last person he would think of being a victim to a crime scene was her.

Shit popping off again, I guess, Benjamin thought as he pulled into his driveway to see Brenda and Renae standing out front watching the scene.

"What's going on?" Benjamin asked his wife as he hugged her and kissed her on her lips.

"Somebody killed Daquan's girlfriend and some boy that nobody knows from Adam and Eve," Renae explained, saying the sententious saying.

"Damn, that's sour!" he retorted.

"And it ain't sweet!" Brenda added.

"Where's Daquan?"

"He's in school, where his ass is supposed to be," Renae answered. "Are you hungry?" she asked while rubbing his stomach.

"Hell, I'm beyond hungry. It depends on what type of food we're . . ."

"Sho' not Ms. Pink. You act like you don't know your Red Sea company," Renae responded, letting Benjamin know that her menstrual cycle was on.

"Damn, baby. Forgive me!" Benjamin said, trying to cheer her up. *Damn, nigga! You slipping!* he thought.

"No, nigga, get with the program. Do it again, and watch how the dog house look for thirty days," Renae joked as she walked into the kitchen.

"Brenda . . ."

"Benjamin, leave me out of that mess!" Brenda quickly said as she texted her boyfriend, Jerome, who was in Canada.

"I see how it is. It's a twin thing, huh?" Benjamin said mockingly.

"No, it's a husband and wife thing. Before I forget, Earl wrote yesterday and said he'll be home to visit soon."

"That's good. How is he?" Benjamin asked.

"Shit! He's in the infantry probably blowing shit up. Only God knows!"

"The kid will be alright," Benjamin said.

"Yeah, I hope so," Brenda said sadly.

"Pancakes, oatmeal, and bacon," Renae informed Brenda and Benjamin of the menu. "Anyone have a problem with that?"

Benjamin looked over at Brenda sitting on the stool at the island and shrugged his shoulders. She simply rolled her eyes and twirled her spoon in her coffee mug.

"Fine with me," Benjamin responded.

"It won't be fine until it gets here," Brenda joked.

"Don't start, Brenda! It's too early in the morning . . ."

While Benjamin sat there and listened to the two twins go back and forth, his mind was on what was going on in the neighborhood.

"Who would want the poor girl dead?" he wanted to know. He'd heard about how she'd given his son gonorrhea. And although it was fucked up, from Benjamin's perspective, the last thing he would ever give thought to was the possibility of his son being the killer.

His mind was on how his son was going to take the news of his girlfriend's death. *I wonder who the fuck did that shit. She was just a sixteen-year-old. Way too damn young to be dying*, Benjamin thought.

* * * * *

It wasn't until the lunch bell sounded that Daquan noticed that the news of Cindy's death had surfaced. A lot of her friends were crying and shouting outside the gym and cafeteria.

"Daquan!" Shaquana called out to her brother as she ran up to him and hugged him, noticing that he was on the verge of breaking down himself.

"It's okay, Daquan. Oh my God! I can't believe this!" Shaquana said, battling back tears herself.

The news had come through Facebook an hour ago, and it produced two photos of two body bags being carried from the apartment. No one knew who the second victim was, and neither did Daquan. All he could remember were the two devils as he pulled the trigger to save his own life.

"This shit can't be real, Sis!" Daquan said, falling to his knees and once again vomiting on the ground.

He was sick to his stomach, and the whole school knew why. They were just far away from knowing who the killer was.

"Daquan Clark, please report to the dean's office immediately," the admissions lady announced over the PA system.

"It's probably Mom or Dad coming to sign you out. Come on, Daquan," Shaquana said as she helped her brother to his feet and walked with him to the dean's office.

When both siblings entered the office, neither of them were staring at their parents.

"Mr. Daquan Clark, my name is Detective Barns, and this is my partner, Detective Lisa Cunningham. We would like to take you down to the station to ask you some questions about your girlfriend, Cindy Mendor, and where you were early this morning."

"I was home in bed . . ."

"Wrong answer, sir, because we have a witness that says otherwise," Detective Barns said.

"Daquan, can you place your hands behind your back. We have to treat every step of the way like a crime, and you are a primary suspect."

"No, ya'll are wrong!" Shaquana screamed hysterically.

"Man, fuck ya'll swines!" Daquan said as he quickly stole on the Detective, who couldn't defend himself from the agility of Daquan's attack. Detective Cunningham removed her Taser gun and hit Daquan with high voltage, bringing him down instantly.

"Nooo! Get off him!" Shaquana yelled as she was restrained by the school resource officer, Mr. Keller.

When Daquan and Shaquana were hauled off campus in handcuffs, the innumerable rumors and speculation began that Daquan killed Cindy out of jealousy, and he and Shaquana killed her together.

F IFTEEN

"My son don't have shit to say to you, motherfuckers!" Benjamin yelled at the detective inside the interrogation room. For hours, Benjamin had been refusing to let the detectives talk to his son. He'd been criticized and called a drug lord who would soon be indicted for every dark name in the book. Despite some of their truths, they had no evidence to prove shit.

And Benjamin knew how not to self-incriminate himself or his son, by simply refusing to talk, which was a right that he had under the constitutional amendments.

"So, you want to tell me . . . instead of clearing your son's name."

"His name is Daquan. What's unclear about that, sir?" Benjamin said, being sardonic with Detective Barns, who had a reputation as a bulldog detective.

This nigger knows his son killed the damn girl. She was cheating on him and gave him an STD. He went to confront her and stumbled across her lover. I need him to get tested for gun residue, Detective Barns thought. He was an eager white man ready to put Daquan and his father away. But like every other hardworking detective in Jonesboro, he needed stronger evidence than circumstantial alone.

"Okay, Mr. Clark, this interrogation is over with. I'm asking you to leave, being you are free to leave. Unfortunately for Daquan, he is under arrest for battery on a law enforcement officer," Detective Barns said, standing up to open the door for Benjamin.

"Son, I don't care what they do or say, you stay quiet. You hear me?" Benjamin said to Daquan.

"Yes, Dad. I hear you," he replied.

"I love you and will be in court tomorrow," Benjamin said as he hugged his son.

"I love you, too, Dad," Daquan retorted.

"You crackers ain't got shit better to do but try fucking up a kid's life?" Benjamin said, looking Barns in his blue eyes.

"What about when a kid takes another kid's life? It's only your kind that does it. Where does that fit into being okay to do?" Detective Barns yelled at Benjamin, who started to chuckle at the perplexity he'd caused Barns—on every attempt to bring him down.

"I have always gotten under your skin, huh? Tell your wife, Beth, that I still have a pole for her, if she wants to start making money again," Benjamin said as he laughed his way out of the station.

Daquan was transported to Jonesboro Juvenile Detention Center, where he was fingerprinted and, unbeknownst to him, tested for gun powder residue. He was tricked into signing for his approval to submit to a gunpowder residue test, because it was set up to make it appear that he was signing for his booking process and orientation papers of the facility rules and regulations. When Daquan's results came back positive, Detective Barns couldn't have been a happier man than he was now.

114

Stupid nigger, he thought as he smiled on his way to a judge to seek out a probable cause search warrant for the home of Daquan Coleman Clark, where the murder weapon was assumed to be.

He was elated as he sped over to the courthouse in his unmarked Yukon SUV. And he had the same feeling that he was accustomed to: success.

"They call me the bulldog, Daquan," Detective Barns exclaimed, blasting Blake Shelton on the radio.

I will not rest until I have all you Clarks in a damn cell or grave, he thought as he navigated the Yukon to the back entrance of the Jonesboro Courthouse.

* * * * *

"Girl, how could they even come to that silly conclusion that Daquan would even do something so stupid like that?" Champagne asked as she comforted Shaquana.

They were at Champagne's house, where she lived with her grandma, who had been her legal guardian since she was three years old. Champagne's parents were both killed in a home invasion by an unknown robber who was after her father, who everyone knew as Big Red. He had Jonesboro on lock with the dope game until Haitian Beny had him killed and hijacked the streets from Big Red.

"Tomorrow he goes to court, and we'll see if the judge lets him come home. They can't punish him for how he reacted by blacking out," Shaquana explained.

"He will be fine. Now please stop stressing," Champagne responded, polishing her toenails a crimson red.

"So, when are you going to see Chad?" Shaquana asked.

"I guess whenever he gets here, but I will be in court tomorrow, Shaquana."

"No school," Shaquana asked.

"Nope!" Champagne answered.

"You know that Maurice called me today."

"What did he want? Ya'll hooking up?" Champagne probed.

"I don't know what he wanted. It was a missed call, and . . . no . . . I'm not hooking up with him. I have a man!" Shaquana replied.

"We're not even about to go there," Champagne retorted with a pout.

"Whatever! I just can't do Donavon like that," Shaquana said, *even though the dick was good*, she thought.

"One of these days, you'll see you're worth better than the stars you see in the sky at night," Champagne said, speaking a sententious proverb.

"He's cute and all, but he's not on time."

"So you'll give him the pussy again?" Champagne asked her.

Shaquana was unaware that Champagne knew of her and Maurice's shower episode before they left the hotel suite.

"I can't even say that!" Shaquana said as she began to blush.

"Bitch, I know you fucked up about him, so you might as well call him!" Champagne insisted.

"Champagne!" Ms. Mae, her grandmother, called out from the living room while sitting in her favorite rocking chair that she never left unoccupied.

"Yes, ma'am!" Champagne called back.

"You have company coming up," Ms. Mae said as she watched Chad pull up in his Chevy Impala SS behind her '93 Volvo.

"Well, I'll see you tomorrow," Shaquana said as she got up to leave.

"Okay, sis. Tell Ma I said hello," Champagne said, speaking of Renae.

"I will," Shaquana retorted.

Before she made her exit, she gave Ms. Mae a warm hug and kiss.

"See you later, Ms. Mae," Shaquana said to the eighty-five-year-old veteran, who was more of a grandmother to her than her own, who was nowhere near as sweet.

"Okay, baby. Be good now!" Ms. Mae called.

When Shaquana walked outside to her Audi, she had no clue that the man inside the Impala SS was thanking her little brother for knocking off one of his enemies. With T-Zoe now dead, all that was left was to go after Maurice, who nobody had seen prior to T-Zoe's death or since.

* * * * *

The nurse, Mrs. Marie, was more than what Tameka had expected, as was the luxurious hotel suite. Marie was a caramel lady, a bit on the heavy side, and in her mid-forties. She took care of Tameka like she was a newborn baby.

"Thank you, Mrs. Marie," Tameka said as Marie placed two new, fluffy comfortable pillows behind her to prop her up.

"It's all good, woman. You will heal in no time. Benjamin knew what he was doing when he called me," Marie said. "Now, let me apply this cream. Be still now . . . and relax," she continued as she gently applied some A+D Ointment to the cuts on Tameka's face.

As Marie finished applying the cream to Tameka's last cut, there were two knocks on the door.

"I'll go get that. Relax yourself," Marie said, tapping her gently on her thighs.

It has to be Benjamin, Tameka thought as Marie walked out of the room to answer the door.

She was elated and feeling like a little girl who was anxious to see her dad.

"Damn, this nigga got me out of my character," she said to herself.

Tameka heard the front door close, followed by Marie walking back inside the room. When she saw the look on Marie's face, she sensed something amiss.

"Is it Benjamin?" Tameka asked Marie, whose bottom lip was trembling.

When Tameka saw the man come into the room with a gun in his hand, her heart dropped in fear of her life.

"Why are you here?" Tameka asked.

"Another time, I'd probably say because of you. But that's not the case. It's Benjamin who I want now!" Jarvis answered.

SIXTEEN

Since learning of Daquan's arrest, Tittyboo hadn't been himself. He knew that the following day Daquan would appear in front of a judge who would give Daquan twenty-one days to serve. In fact, he knew the routine well himself, since he had been incarcerated in a juvenile facility.

I was stupid for letting him get the gun, Tittyboo thought, regretting his fatal mistake.

Not knowing where the gun was bothered Tittyboo because the bullets had his prints on them as did the gun.

Where the fuck is that gun? Tittyboo thought to himself as Shay walked into the living room in her boy shorts and satin bra. She climbed on top of his lap and put her arms around his neck.

"What's wrong with you, baby?" she asked, taking the blunt from his mouth and inhaling the flakka into her lungs. "Thinking about your boy?" she retorted, simultaneously exhaling the smoke from her nostrils and mouth.

"I just hope my lil' nigga alright," Tittyboo said.

"Honestly, baby, I don't think Daquan hurt Cindy," Shay exclaimed.

"Why is everybody putting him in that shit? He isn't locked up for that, and my boy is no O.J. Simpson!" Tittyboo shouted, defending his homeboy's reputation.

Killing a nigga about a bitch is what suckas do. I'll never place him in that category, he thought.

"Baby, I just don't want you stressing," Shay said as she kissed him on his lips. Feeling the flakka kicking in, she slid down seductively to Tittyboo's crotch and reached into his Gucci sweatpants. She grabbed hold of his semi-erect penis, passionately stroking him to a full erection before placing him in her mouth and sucking him like her favorite lollipop.

"Damn, baby. That shit feels good!" he moaned out while blowing a cloud of flakka and marijuana smoke into her face.

"Umm!" she moaned in ecstasy as she slurped on his dick. Shay was one of those women who came to an orgasm by just giving a man head.

"And from the sound of her moans, Tittyboo knew that she'd come to her first one.

Not wanting to spend all her time on her knees, she pulled down Tittyboo's sweatpants around his ankles and took off her moist boy shorts. She then climbed back into his lap, stood up and put her hands on his shoulders, and slowly descended on his love stick.

"Uhh!" she moaned as he filled her womb.

"Damn, baby!" Tittyboo softly moaned out as Shay gyrated her hips and rode him rapidly.

"Uh! Uh! Uh!" her moans intensified the more she came down on him.

Smack!

I love this bitch! Tittyboo thought as he slapped her on her ass cheeks.

Together they transformed, from the intoxication of the flakka, into supernatural lovers who were on their own dimensional planes.

* * * * *

"So, you don't think that it's possible for your son to have slumped the girl and boy?" Percy Green said to Benjamin as he sat in his favorite chair on the porch of his antique house.

"Anything is possible!" Benjamin said, sitting on the edge of the porch swinging his legs.

Old man Percy Green lived out in the woods of Savanna and was Benjamin's mentor as well as his connect. It was Percy who made it possible for Benjamin to master the dope game. The reason Benjamin had no mansion or million-dollar cars on his lawn was because he had heeded Percy's advice. Percy was connected to the Mexican cartel through marriage and blood relations. Never being a fan of luxury materials, he faithfully managed to stay under the radar from the feds. He owned a couple of acres of land throughout Savanna, but nothing conspicuous or preposterous that would alert the feds. Percy was in his mid-eighties and lived alone as a widow, except for Spot, his malamute husky.

"Son, sometimes in life you have to make what seems impossible, possible," Percy began, breaking the shells of his roasted peanuts and eating them. Spot walked up onto the porch and laid down at his heels

"You're right, old man. It's just . . ."

"You don't want to imagine your son being behind the gun that killed that girl, and it's understandable. But to do that means to risk saving him if you could, Benjamin," Percy said.

Benjamin looked back at Percy and knew that the old man was correct.

"Always have an opposite perspective from walking in your shoes into the shoes of the FBI. The same goes for the killer's shoes," Percy retorted as he stood up out of the rocking chair and slowly walked inside his home, slamming the screen door.

"He's right. It's 3:00 in the morning, and other than being out here for my drop and to drop his money off, I was asking for advice. How would the police see it? Damn, Son!" Benjamin exclaimed as he jumped from the porch, now being led by his instincts. "Percy, I have to go. I will come get that in the morning!" Benjamin continued as he hastened over to his burgundy Explorer and rashly sped away from Percy's home, kicking up dirt the entire mile-long road.

I knew that you'd soon come to your senses, Son. Think like the killer . . . like the dope man is supposed to think, like the feds, Percy thought as he stood behind his screen door and watched Benjamin's taillights vanish into the night.

"Get in here, Spot!" Percy said as he opened the door to let inside his best friend.

Once Spot was in the house, Percy closed the front door and went to store the $2 million that Benjamin brought with him in his secret hidden safe that was installed under the bathtub in his bathroom. In fact, only he, Spot, and God knew the safe existed.

* * * * *

Renae and Shaquana were both in the kitchen drinking hot chocolate when the front door came down with a battering ram, which caused a loud impact and scared the women to death.

"Jonesboro police . . . get down on the ground!" Detective Barns yelled, holding his gun in front of him while searching for targets. More than a dozen police arrived wearing raid gear and carrying M-16 rifles. They swarmed the home in search of targets.

"Oh my God, Shaquana. Baby, get down!" Renae told her daughter timorously.

"Get down now!" Detective Barns screamed as he swept his gun toward the kitchen and found two of his targets, who were complying with his orders.

Where the fuck is Benjamin? he thought, preferring to catch him so that he could unload his weapon into him. That would be the only way to end it . . . a wrongful yet justified death. But unfortunately for Detective Barns, Benjamin was nowhere in the home.

"Clear upstairs," a police officer said.

"Put them in restraints and execute the search warrant. I want this place destroyed . . . and I mean destroyed!" Detective Barns said emphatically.

"You have no right to come into our home like this!" Renae screamed.

"Bitch, shut the fuck up! Now get her out of my face . . . both of them!" Barns yelled, nonchalantly blowing Renae off with his hand.

* * * * *

"Damn!" Benjamin exclaimed as he pulled up to his house and saw innumerable police cars. There was a variety of unmarked cars and Jonesboro police cruisers. Making a dash from the Explorer toward the front door, he was stopped short by being tackled and handcuffed behind his back by two bouncer-sized officers.

"Man, what the fuck going on?" Benjamin yelled, already knowing the looks of a search warrant. They knew him too well to be searching for drugs.

Benjamin had outsmarted some of the best narcotics agents in the police department for the longest time. *They are here for one thing . . . and, God, I hope it wasn't here*, Benjamin thought as he listened to the sounds of his home being ransacked by the police.

"We meet again . . . just on another set, Mr. Clark!" Detective Barns walked outside saying while staring directly into Benjamin's eyes.

In his hand, he held up a clear plastic bag that contained a black .357 revolver.

"So, tell me, Benjamin. Do you still say that Daquan didn't commit this crime? I can bet you all of your drug money that this is the same gun that killed those two lovers!" Barns told Benjamin, who was speechless and now appeared hurt.

"Let him go. We've found what we came for," Barns said before he stormed off toward his unmarked car.

The bulldog has found the bone, Barns thought, elated as he sped away from the Clark's residence with the murder weapon.

SEVENTEEN

Daquan walked through the side door of the courtroom, wearing a yellow jumpsuit with the word "juvenile" stamped on the back in big black letters. He was shackled at his ankles, handcuffed in front, and had a belly chain placed around his waist. As he surveyed the room for his mother, he saw the veteran detective who wanted him to talk. As they sat him in the jury box with other juvenile inmates, the doors opened, and his family and friends stepped inside. He was happy to see his mother, father, sister, Auntie Brenda, and Champagne. But the looks on their faces left him bothered.

"Hey, baby!" Renae whispered to him from the audience while drying her eyes with a tissue. They were prohibited from talking to him, and they were limited to only so much body language.

Why is everyone looking so hurt? This is my first time being incarcerated. My cellmate told me that I would get a slap on my wrist and get released today, Daquan thought while swinging side to side in the comfortable chair.

"All cell phones need to be shut off while in the courtroom. In approximately five minutes, the Honorable Judge Robert Cowell will be in session," the old white bailiff announced to everyone.

TWO MASKS ONE HEART

The bailiff was a chubby old man in his late seventies, who spoke with great seniority. However, everyone knew him as Mr. Ku Klux Klan, who had more potency than the state attorneys.

When the doors opened again, Daquan and everyone else turned their heads and watched a tall black man walk in wearing an expensive black suit and surveying the room. It was evident that he was looking for someone in particular.

I wonder whose dad that is. He looks like a million bucks! Daquan thought as he watched the man strut over to his father from behind and whisper in his ear.

He knows Dad . . . whoever's dad he is! Daquan thought, making eye contact with Shaquana, who was lip-talking to him. Whatever she was trying to tell him was incomprehensible, for he was not equipped for reading lips. Whatever she was saying formed butterflies in his stomach and made him think of Cindy.

It also didn't take long for the news to hit the population in the detention center of who the dude was at Cindy's apartment. He'd never heard of T-Zoe before and quickly learned that he was from College Park.

What is she trying to tell me? Daquan was perplexed as the bailiff announced the judge's presence.

"All rise for Honorable Robert Cowell of the 3rd Circuit Court of Jonesboro, Georgia. This court is now in session. Could you please be seated and give your undivided attention to Honorable Judge Robert Cowell," the bailiff concluded.

As everyone took their seats, two state attorneys, both women in their fifties, walked through a side door.

"Devils!" a juvenile inmate seated next to Daquan whispered to those in his vicinity.

The two women were both hefty and impassive to juveniles who broke the law. Their names were Catherine Styles and Christina Jones. Thirty seconds later, all of the public defenders entered through another side door and seated themselves at a long table opposite from the state attorneys.

"I would like to call Ryan Smith of case number C-J2013," Judge Cowell said into the microphone.

Ryan strutted from the jury box to the podium, escorted by the bailiff, where his public defender awaited him.

"Is this your client?" Judge Cowell asked Ryan's attorney, Ms. Smith, who was a beautiful blonde in her mid-thirties and resembled Paris Hilton.

"Yes, Your Honor."

"And are you Ryan Smith?" the judge asked him.

"Yeah, that's me . . ."

"What a coincidence to have the same last name. Any relation?" the judge asked, looking down at Ms. Smith, with his glasses on the bridge of his nose.

"No, sir. There's no relation," Ms. Smith retorted.

Judge Cowell was a short, stubby white man in his seventies, who was known as an angel from heaven because he gave juveniles a break more often than he incarcerated them.

"Catherine, could you please read me the facts of this case?" Judge Cowell asked of the state. She already had Ryan's file in her hands.

"Your Honor . . . Ryan Smith," she began as she walked toward the judge and handed him a copy of the exact same file in her hands. "He is a frequent offender who was arrested for possession of marijuana and breaking his 7:00 p.m. curfew. The state is asking for Ryan Smith to be sentenced to a juvenile program, one that would help rehabilitate him and show him discipline," Catherine continued, in an irksome, squeaky voice.

"And how long are you suggesting Ryan Smith stay in this program?" the judge asked.

"Six months," Catherine answered.

"Anything the lawyer of the defendant has to say?"

"Yes, sir. We will object to him going to a program, because the defendant is seventeen years old."

"When will he be eighteen?" Judge Cowell followed.

"Next month, sir," Ms. Smith responded.

"Ryan Smith . . . I sentence you to twenty-one days to serve in a juvenile facility. Normally I wouldn't override my state's suggestions, but sending him away would be useless. If I could send you away and be sure that it would teach you, you'd be going," the judge said to Ryan.

For the next hour and a half, the judge called every juvenile case until he finally got to Daquan.

"Daquan Coleman Clark . . . please approach."

About time, Daquan thought as he was being escorted to the podium by the bailiff like everyone else.

Daquan watched the tall black man in the expensive suit pass through the gate from the audience and come stand next to him. It was evident to everyone and now Daquan that the man was his lawyer.

"Are you Daquan, sir?" Judge Cowell asked.

"Yes, sir!" Daquan answered.

"State . . . read," the judge demanded.

Instead of Catherine reading the file to the judge, Christina decided to handle seeking punishment for Daquan.

"Your Honor, Daquan is a murder suspect and is being sought out for an indictment as we speak. On the other hand, he is a first-time offender, so his score is in the lows. But we still want him to be held at least twenty-one days due to the possible indictment," she said.

"Anything from the defendant's lawyer?"

"Yes, sir," Mr. Goodman said in a smooth, laid-back voice.

"This is my client's first time being in trouble. And I would like the facts of this case to be considered, Your Honor," he said, pausing to pull a paper from his folder.

Everyone watched as he strutted over to the judge and handed over a copy that he was about to present.

"Sir, that is a photo of a Facebook news report of the defendant's deceased girlfriend when it went public," the judge said. "Sir, shortly after my client saw this same photo, two detectives approached him and accused him of hurting his girlfriend. So it was a heat of passion outburst. I'm requesting that my cliet be released to his family on house arrest, sir, instead of remaining incarcerated," Mr. Goodman suggested.

"Your Honor, the state would like to as well bring it to the court's attention that we find reason to believe that releasing him would be a threat to society. The indictment evidently wouldn't be handled in juvenile court, sir. But it is a good faith act to hold him until further notice," Christina exclaimed.

Man, I can't believe this shit! These motherfuckers trying me like a suspect, and I ain't even charge for the shit! Daquan thought.

"State . . . what convincing evidence could you give me to believe he is a threat?" Judge Cowell asked Christina.

"Sir, a search warrant was executed at the defendant's home . . ."

Oh shit! Daquan thought, with a stomach full of butterflies and perspiration forming on his upper lip and forehead.

"And a weapon was found that is believed to be the murder weapon."

Damn! Daquan thought as Christina walked toward the judge and handed him a copy of the search warrant and murder weapon—a photo that sealed his fate.

"Daquan Coleman Clark . . . I sentence you to twenty-one days to serve in a juvenile facility," the judge said.

There was no way that he was going to release me now. They've found the gun! Daquan thought as he walked through the side door, never looking back at his disappointed family.

EIGHTEEN

"Ahh shit, Ben!" she moaned as he pumped in and out of her excessive wetness. Her back was arched while gripping the edge of his desk.

"Damn, Benjamin! Beat this pussy!" she moaned, feeling him deeply in her womb.

She knew the stress that he was going through with the possibility of his son being charged with a murder. So she made it her business to ditch her man and homegirl to come assuage her everything. The more he fucked her, the more her feelings for him increased. She loved him and desperately wanted to become a new replacement in his life. But she knew well of the obstruction in her path: Renae.

She'd thought of all the mischievous ways to get Renae out of the picture, and they all came back full circle to the same evil conclusion.

Renae has to die . . . and I will be there to support him through his grief, like I am now, she thought as she came to her climax, presenting a heavy load of her cream flow.

"Uhh! Yes, Daddy! I love you!" she moaned out as Benjamin came himself, sending his seeds though her love tunnel and to her nest.

With a baby, there would be no return, she thought as she laced her legs around his waist and brought him down to kiss him passionately.

"Girl! I don't know what I'm going to do with you," Benjamin said as he looked her in her hypnotic eyes.

"You'll keep me by your side through the good and bad days. I love you, Benjamin."

He knew that the words she spoke were true, and the way he felt for her was ineffable love. He respected how she played her position, and one thing he couldn't deny was how true his love was.

"I love you too, beautiful. Now let's get our clothes on. I have to run to a meeting in a few," Benjamin said as he wiped himself off with a towel.

"Okay!" she said, jumping off the desk and sliding back into her Macy's red dress and heels.

They both could hear Antron recording in the background, which meant that more eyes had come to the studio. But the last thing that anyone would expect was their secretive relationship. As she came to give him a kiss before leaving, a thought came to his mind.

"Baby, are you still taking the birth control?" he asked her with concern after realizing that he'd once again rebelled against pulling out. The last thing he needed was for her to come up pregnant from him. So many lives would be affected.

"Of course I am, Daddy. I don't need no kids right now," she retorted untruthfully. The sooner that she became pregnant, the sooner her plan could be more effective.

By all means, she had plans to get Renae out of the picture. And like every crab in the bucket that pulls the others down, she was unaware that she was mistress number two—because someone else wanted Benjamin's heart . . . and Renae's disappearance.

* * * * *

Seeing his homeboy laid to rest in the open casket had given him a reality check. Maurice knew that claiming the streets meant to be taken by them when the time came. He had made enough money to step away from the game and do something extraordinary with his cash.

"These streets were never promised to us, T-Zoe . . . that's why you were supposed to enjoy it while it was good. If you would have come with me to the Lil' Boosie concert, then you would have had your chance to fuck Champagne. But I fucked them both for us, homeboy. I can't even question why you were in Jonesboro, and the shit I'm hearing ain't good, shawty. The bitch was only sixteen . . . way too young and not worth your life. Now you see why I put war before money . . . and pussy before money—because you never know when it will all end," Maurice said to T-Zoe lying in the casket, the color of ebony, with a Haitian flag folded neatly on his chest.

Unlike Cindy, T-Zoe had a private funeral service at the funeral home that prepared him for a proper burial. He left behind his one true friend and a small family of brothers and sisters.

"Well, shawty, it's time for me to go. Keep your eyes open for my enemies," Maurice said as he kissed his homeboy on his forehead.

When Maurice turned around to leave, he met eyes with Haitian Beny and his two bodyguards.

Man, what the fuck he doing here? Maurice thought as he walked out of the room and funeral home altogether.

"So, you just going to walk past me, huh?" Beny asked Maurice as he and his two men walked outside behind him.

Maurice stopped in his tracks and turned around with a frown on his face. He knew why Haitian Beny was eager to see him, but unfortunately for Beny, Maurice had nothing for him. It was because of his manufacturing that a drug war was going on in College Park.

I remember a time where everyone ate (hustled) on the same block; now it is all competitive and converted to niggas killing niggas, Maurice thought.

"What's up, Beny?" Maurice asked, watching all three men for any false moves. He was ready to die trying, never being one to leave home without some form of automatic.

"I know that you're going through a stage of grief, and trust me, I understand. But you know how it is out here . . ."

"I don't need you to remind me, shawty. I hold my own out here. That's why I'm still standing," Maurice said, not wanting to hear no man give him a lecture about the streets.

"So you do know it well, and if that's the case, then there shall be no problem paying the dead man's tab," Beny said.

"So, that's why you are here . . . to step to me about a dead man's tab," Maurice retorted, getting red in the face.

"Actually, I'm here to sell the dead man's tab, by asking a favor from you . . . one that could compensate for what T-Zoe owes me already," Beny said as he pulled a cigar from a golden case and put flame to it.

"How much do a dead man owe anybody?" Maurice said, being sardonic.

Haitian Beny took a pull from his cigar, blew the smoke into Maurice's face, and said, "So we going to play them games, huh?"

"Since when a nigga getting killed in these streets become a game?" Maurice shot back with a question.

"Listen, Son. We never plan to die in these streets when we join them . . . and that's the problem. T-Zoe was a good connect."

"Then why put him on top and not tell us what the fuck got these junkies out of control?" Maurice fired at Beny, wanting to know the ingredients to the whip game that had so much blood in the streets.

"Maurice, that's none of your concern, how I make mine. Your job is to get me my money. It's $3.5 million out there with my name on it . . . !"

"What? 3.5 million? What the fuck you take me for?" Maurice exclaimed at the preposterous debt that Beny claimed T-Zoe owed him.

"I take you for a nigga that knows how this shit work . . . and not no nigga who feel the need to die about it . . ."

"We all going to die nig . . . ," Maurice attempted to say as he stepped back and pulled out his Glock .40. However, he was impressed at the agility of Big Funk and Corey, who had two guns a piece aimed at him.

Damn these niggas. We'll all die! Maurice thought as he trained his gun from Big Funk to Corey, with growing perspiration appearing on his forehead and upper lips, despite the cool atmosphere and young night.

"If I would have bet my money that you wouldn't react like this, then I would have lost. But getting you to understand that no one out here gives a fuck about dying is the catch-22. You pull, and we'll pull harder. Now being that you done backed yourself into a sticky situation, I know that I have your undivided attention now. T-Zoe was a good friend of mine, and despite his debt, I want the real person responsible for his death. He goes by the name of Benjamin Clark. Make him history, and I'll have an irresistible position waiting for you that's more than what a dead man could ever have . . . !"

"Who says I'm down for hits?" Maurice asked.

"The moment you raised that gun made you an employee under me. You have a job to do, and I want it done within the next ninety days," Haitian Beny demanded, blowing smoke into Maurice's face. He then turned away to walk from his presence with his two bodyguards.

Maurice still had his gun aimed at all their backs. He had the opportunity to squeeze his Glock empty; however, he chose not to. He lowered his weapon from the backs of the three fearless men.

We all gotta die someday, but obviously, none of us chose to die today, he thought. He had no clue of how he would pull off the formidable task when his heart was crying to be accepted by the man's daughter.

This is the part of life that becomes difficult, Maurice thought as he hopped on the interstate on his way to Jonesboro.

NINETEEN

Through all the sudden drama in his life, dealing with Daquan's issue and hyping up the security around him and the club, Benjamin had finally gotten a chance to return to the beautiful woman that he was reviving back to life. As he pulled up to the Hilton hotel, he was like a nervous kid, anxious to be in school the next day, just to sit with the beautiful girl that he had a crush on.

Before exiting his Jaguar, he showered himself in some of his Polo cologne.

"Now that's how a man is supposed to smell. Now let's keep it pimping," Benjamin said as he emerged from the car with a dozen red roses in his hand.

Last time I tried this, I had to save my baby. I know she looking better and most definitely feeling better, he thought as he walked inside the luxurious hotel lobby. As he walked toward the elevators, he was stopped by a familiar female employee.

"Um, Mr. Clark, I have a confidential letter for you . . . from Mrs. Marie," the beautiful young brunette named Francelina said.

"Is everything okay, baby girl?" Benjamin asked, sensing something amiss.

"It's confidential, sir. I was told to give it to you when I saw you, and to let you know that both women really appreciated your kindness," Francelina told him as she walked back toward the front desk with Benjamin on her heels.

He watched her go into the back and quickly return with a concealed white envelope. As she handed it to him, he immediately recognized the feminine handwriting.

"Thanks," Benjamin said, walking away back toward the elevator while tearing open the envelope.

"Um, Mr. . . . ."

"What now, woman?" he retorted in a whisper.

"Mr. Clark. They are no longer listed with us, sir . . ."

"What? Where did they go?" Benjamin asked in bewilderment while pulling the letter out to read:

When you thought that you had me beat, you risked your life when you swapped out your much-needed strength. Now you have to protect your most vulnerable piece. Thought that you could hide her, huh? And we both know that it's not Renae nor "Dom Pérignon." At fifteen, I thought that I had a real dad, but he let a stripper come between us. Love always, your son.

"Damn it!" Benjamin exclaimed, with fire in his eyes. He looked around for the girl, Francelina, but she was now busy with a customer at the front desk.

Damn it, Jarvis! Damn it! he thought as he stormed out the exit door.

"I will kill this nigga!" Benjamin yelled out, throwing the roses to the ground and sprinting to his car. As he burnt

140

rubber out of the Hilton hotel parking lot, he had one thing on his mind . . . going to the same destination.

"If he has laid a hand on her, I swear I will kill him," Benjamin said as he accelerated on the interstate on his way to Bankhead, where he knew he'd find Jarvis.

* * * * *

"Why are you not eating, Donavon?" Shaquana asked him while he was playing with his food.

To be honest, I'm disinterested in you, Ms. Beautiful. The signs seem clear as daylight. You are not Berlinda! Donavon so badly wanted to say to Shaquana. But instead, he removed his gold-rimmed glasses from his face, placed them on the table, and said, "I'm worried about my future, Shaquana."

They were at a nice Italian restaurant in Atlanta, spending some much-needed quality time together. It was their first time since he stood her up two times after the Bossie concert that they had the chance to be together. She observed earlier that something was on his mind, but she was far from making any suggestions that she was the problem. She wiped the spaghetti sauce from her mouth with a napkin and gave him her undivided attention.

Damn, she's gorgeous, but why can I no longer be affected by her sex appeal? Donavon wanted to know.

Because she will never be like Berlinda, you dolt! his inner voice retorted to him.

"What seems to be the problem, baby?" Shaquana asked Donavon, whose thoughts were oozing from his head.

141

He wanted badly to inform her of the double life that he'd been living, but he couldn't find the words.

"I never thought that law school would be so stressful!" Donavon said while massaging his temples and eye sockets.

"Baby, to get good results, you have to put in good work and effort. Isn't that what my daddy tells us all the time?"

"Yeah, he does, and I know that, but we're living in a time where principle doesn't relinquish the anguish of becoming a black lawyer. And honestly, I'm not trying to sound reprehensive; it's just starting to wear down on me," Donavon said as he fluctuated his real frustration and converted to a feigned burdensome problem.

"Listen, Donavon, I can't express in words how happy I am for you. You have to remember where you're predestined to be."

I came from out of the darkness in a closet, and can't tell you like a man that I'm a fuckin' homosexual, he wanted to tell her. But like always, he decided to keep his double love life to himself.

"I love you, Donavon, and together we could do it . . ."

You are not Berlinda, his inner voice said.

"I love you too, baby," Donavon retorted, far from meaning it. He loved only one person more than himself, and Shaquana was nowhere near being Berlinda.

She loves me, but does she love me beyond limitations to accept me for who I am? Donavon thought.

"Do you love me beyond limitations, Shaquana?" he asked curiously.

"My love for you, Donavon, is ineffable, so no . . . there are no limits. One day I want to be able to marry you and have your kids, Donavon. I love you to the moon and back!" Shaquana said, reaching across the table rubbing his hand passionately, showing him that she really cared for him like no other.

She would always think of the day that she gave him the chance to break her virginity. Everyone in the school called him a sophisticated nerd, and it was her chance to score something different from the others by making him her boyfriend. Falling in love with each other as the days went by was inevitable for the both. She did her best to shoot Donavon a curveball on marriage, but he was too caught up on him and Berlinda to catch it.

"No limits, right?" Donavon asked sincerely.

"No limits, Donavon!" She retorted.

* * * * *

They couldn't keep their hands off of each other as they made their way to his suite. Once inside, Shaquana jumped into Donavon's arms and felt his hands inevitably slide up her Tom Ford mini dress. With her arms wrapped around his neck, she kissed him deep and passionately while being carried to the bedroom and laid on the soft, comfortable king-sized bamboo canopy bed.

"Donavon!" she moaned out as he sucked on her neck, knowing her sensitive spot. For some reason, she felt that he would give his best performance tonight.

143

The energy that he was feeding off would hurt her if she knew. Together they helped each other out of their clothes and let love be love. Kissing her body from head to toe until he met her hairless plump love tunnel was all part of the plan he had for her. He blindfolded her so that every step of the way would be a surprise for her. As he sucked and licked on her clitoris, Shaquana's moans intensified.

"Uhh! Donavon, yes!" Shaquana yelled out, gyrating her hips as he made love to her with his tongue.

"Damn, he's doing his thang tonight. This sh . . . !"

When she felt Donavon tongue-twirling on her asshole, she let out a moan distinct from the others. Shaquana pulled her legs back toward her head to allow him better access. Her flexibility helped facilitate the new foreplay.

Damn! This nigga eats my ass better than my pussy. We have to do this more often, Shaquana thought.

"Hold on, baby!" Donavon said.

"Okay, baby!" she exclaimed, breathless.

Donavon reached over and went into his nightstand to remove a tube of KY jelly. He quickly lubricated himself and then applied a sufficient amount on Shaquana's asshole.

What the fuck is that? she wanted to know, perplexed from the distinctness of it being Donavon's tongue. Despite her perplexity, she continued to moan out in ecstasy, for it was feeling too good to inquire about. When she felt his finger slide into her asshole, her body trembled from an electrifying wave of ecstasy.

"Oh damn! That shit feels good, Donavon!" she moaned while rubbing her clitoris.

"Get on all fours and put that ass in the air!" Donavon demanded of Shaquana.

She immediately did as she was ordered. She knew that Donavon enjoyed taking her from the back and that it was her favorite position. She felt that a man was more in control when a woman was ass up and face down.

"Like this baby?" *Smack!* Shaquana asked seductively, slapping her ass to entice Donavon.

"No limits, right?"

Why keep asking me that? Shaquana wanted to know, but instead responded, "No limits, Donavon."

When she told him what he wanted to hear, he spread both her ass cheeks apart and shoved his erect love tool inside her lubricated asshole.

"Ahh! Nooo! Take it out! Take it out!" Shaquana screamed hysterically, trying to get away from the painful strokes. But she was unable to escape the grip that Donavon had on her hips.

"It hurts, Donavon! It hurts," she cried out, feeling her skin rip from his enormous size.

But Donavon was gone in his mind, unable to hear her cries. She pulled the sheets off the front of his bed and clawed at the mattress, causing her to break her manicured nails.

I can't believe he's doing this me! Shaquana thought as the pain subsided and converted into pleasure.

"Uhh! Uhh! Donavon!" she moaned. She took note of how long Donavon was lasting and gave him some points. *I can't believe this. All it took was a shot of ass*, she thought as Donavon penetrated her deep as he could go, but with Berlinda on his mind.

"Donavon! Oh shit! I'm cumming!" Shaquana yelled out unconsciously, using her asshole muscles that caused Donavon to explode.

"Arrgghhhh, Berlinda!" he shouted out, realizing that he spoke his thoughts out loud.

Who the fuck is Berlinda? Shaquana wanted to know as the inevitable tears cascaded down her face.

When he came out of her, she hastened to the bathroom and locked the door. Falling to the ground, she cried hysterically.

It was all a lie! Neither one of us loved each other. How did it get like this? she asked herself.

"Shaquana, baby, I'm sorry. Open up the door. I can explain!" Donavon said as he banged on the bathroom door.

When he saw that she wasn't breaking, he went back into the room and collapsed on the bed. She didn't deserve to be left in the dark. *I have to tell her about my double life,* Donavon thought as he drifted off to sleep.

When he awoke, Shaquana was gone . . . and so was their relationship—but not on their decisions. Love could be broken and forgiving, but Mother Nature had her own way of perpetual healing.

T WENTY

B enjamin was never the type to run into a trap headfirst. For a long time, he'd been laying niggas to rest, always moving with a strategic plan. He and Big Dee sat in a black Suburban a block down from where Jarvis's car was parked in the street. The neighborhood was a middle-class area, with various races of families who could afford the $1,200 a month rent. Benjamin and Big Dee had been watching the house all night until dawn, where every living creature could be revealed. Together, they maintained surveillance like the FBI would do.

I know she's in there, Benjamin thought while looking through a set of binoculars.

"Shawty, watch the young'n," Big Dee said as he watched the young boy pull up to Jarvis's trap on a bicycle and go straight to the backyard.

"He's coming to feed the dogs," Benjamin retorted, knowing beforehand that the boy would show up every morning. Jarvis owned ten blue-nose pit bulls and had the young boy, Jamar, come every morning to feed and care for them.

He is too smart to make it look so simple, Benjamin thought, considering Jarvis's intelligence.

Benjamin pulled out his iPhone and dialed Jarvis's number on speaker phone, getting him to answer the phone on the third ring.

"Hello?" a female voice answered, that Benjamin knew to be Tameka.

"Tameka, baby girl. Are you okay?" Benjamin asked out of concern.

"What have I done for this to happen to me, Ben? He's going to . . ."

Smack!

"Uhhh!"

The sound of Tameka being slapped and in pain sent Benjamin's blood pressure shooting up.

"Damn it, Jarvis! Why?" Benjamin barked with emotion in his voice that revealed his hurt.

"Why? How about you ask yourself that?" Jarvis retorted.

"So we really got to go through this Jarvis?"

"Man, you took the *we* out of us, remember? Now you want to pay attention, huh?"

"Nigga! Fuck you and what you have to say!"

"You want this ho, right? Then do what I need to be done. You don't fire no one from the game, shawty. They either retire or die, and since you retired me, then I need my retirement funds, shawty . . ."

"So this about money, huh?" Benjamin asked.

"It's been about money the moment you chose pussy before loyalty . . . Remember? Or you got amnesia, nigga?

How about I make you remember, nigga?" Jarvis screamed out in rage.

Smack!

"Uhhh!

Smack!

"Uhhh! Please!"

Smack!

"Uhhh!"

"You remember now?" Jarvis screamed out as the cries of Tameka could be heard, evident from the sounds of her being slapped around.

Benjamin closed his eyes and could only imagine what Tameka was going through. It was all because of him that her life was now on the line, and he saw no other option but to man up and save her from the perilous situation.

"So, what's up, Benjamin? Are you going to abandon her like you did me, or come like the big man you are? I don't blame Haitian Beny for coming after your head, Ben. Because when I dismissed him, you reinstated him. I don't want your streets, Benjamin. I want what I work hard for, nigga. I've risked my life on many occasions and worked my ass off . . . to be betrayed!"

Smack!

"Awww!" Tameka screamed.

"Damn it, son! Do we have to do this?" Benjamin yelled at Jarvis, unable to sit and listen to him torture her.

"Of course! It's going to be like this, unless there's a better way, nigga!" Jarvis exclaimed, sounding like he was possessed by a demon.

"What do you want, Jarvis, for both of them? You know Marie is as innocent as Majik. Jarvis . . . please don't hurt them!" Benjamin pleaded.

"Benjamin, I'ma tell you this one time. The next time I pick this phone up, I will be hearing numbers. Do we understand each other?" Jarvis asked.

"Please, Ben . . . !"

"Bitch, shut up!"

Smack! Smack! Smack!

"Awww!"

"Jarvis . . . son. No more, okay? Keep your hands off of her, son!" Benjamin yelled into the iPhone hysterically.

"I want my half of our hard-worked fortune, Ben. I have two offshore accounts that I will text you the numbers of when we hang up. You have seventy-two hours to wire $4.5 million to each account. When that is done, you'll see this bitch walk alive at our designated location. To keep good faith and good business, Benjamin, I will let Marie walk now," Jarvis explained before disconnecting the call.

Wow, $4.5 each. That's 9 flat! He knew I'm worth more, but he chose to hit low. This is what I created, Benjamin thought as he sat in silence.

"Yo, that's Marie, I'm guessing," Big Dee said while looking at the heavyset woman in nurse scrubs, looking like she was lost.

"Yeah! That's her," Benjamin stated as he started the Suburban and drove down to pick up Mrs. Marie.

When he pulled in front of her, he let down the passenger window so she could see that it was him. Marie's face lit up with joy when she saw Benjamin.

"Come on, Marie. Let me get you home," Benjamin promised while looking at the front door of Jarvis's house. Benjamin stared Jarvis directly in his eyes while he held a gun to Tameka's head. He could see duct tape around her mouth . . . and a stream of tears cascading down her battered face.

"Three days," Jarvis mouthed off to Benjamin before he closed the curtains to the front office.

When Mrs. Marie was safely inside, Benjamin pulled off.

"Mrs. Marie, sorry for all of this. I will make sure that this will never occur again."

"It's okay, Benjamin. I'm alive, and no one has hurt me. You don't have to worry yourself. Just do what you have to do to save that girl, okay?" Marie said.

"I will, Mrs. Marie. If it's to give my life, I will. She's not my wife, but she doesn't deserve to lose her life because of me!" Benjamin exclaimed as his iPhone received a text.

"Switzerland," Benjamin said to himself as he looked at the two separate offshore accounts that Jarvis had texted him. He had to be careful to move $9 million and continue to stay under the radar.

"Big Dee, I'ma need you to run the club tonight, and handle Jacksonville for me," Benjamin announced.

"I got your back, Ben. You know that," Big Dee retorted.

In the back seat, Mrs. Marie looked at Benjamin and couldn't help but smile and be grateful for knowing Benjamin Clark.

He is my hero and meal ticket out of Atlanta, Marie thought, anxious to touch the new fruits of her life.

* * * * *

"What do you mean, Berlinda? She's gone, and we're no longer together," Donavon said to Berlinda, who had just ended their relationship and their last time having sex.

"Donavon, this has nothing to do with her. It's just not going to work, boo . . ."

"What the fuck you mean?" Donavon screamed, jumping fully nude from the bed and running up on Berlinda, who was fixing his Beyoncé wig.

"Why, Berlinda, huh?" he asked as he spun Berlinda around by his wide shoulders, being splenetic.

"You wanted me to leave her for a damn good reason. I love you, Berlinda, and this is what I get?" Donavon cried out, with tears in his eyes.

Berlinda didn't know how to tell Donavon that he had found a new lover in LA. His lover wanted him to leave Donavon and move to California with him, and Berlinda said that it would be done. To show his new lover that he was submissive, he was leaving Donavon today.

"Listen, Donavon. It's over! Like I said, it's not you. I'm involved with . . ."

Smack!

Before Berlinda could get the words out, Donovan quickly backhanded him.

"I've taken a lot of those, Donavon. Is that all?"

Bop! Bop!

Donavon's second attempt to slap Berlinda resulted in him being laid out on the floor, nude and unconscious, from Berlinda's weave and two-piece combination.

"Bitch, I know kung fu, nigga," Berlinda said, grabbing his Louis Vuitton bag, keys, and heels all at once before leaving Donavon's world for good.

When Donavon gained his consciousness, he felt a sharp pain in his jaw and realized that both his jaw and glasses were shattered to pieces—along with his life. Getting up from the ground, he walked over to his nightstand, removed his loaded .357, and shoved it in his mouth. There was only one way to end the pain—and it was over with as he pulled the trigger.

Boom!

T WENTY-ONE

Every night was a nightmare for Daquan. The day he came back from court he got into a brawl with his cellmate for accusing him of being a liar. Most of the juvenile inmates saw that Daquan was very splenetic. So they stayed out of his way and never asked him to participate in any of the activities with them. He was fearless and was called an animal by the antagonistic guards.

He was standing in line once again to use the phone when he saw a white boy dialing out again discreetly. Never being the one to talk, Daquan skipped the black boy who was next behind the white boy and hung up the white boy's phone

"Hey, man, what are you doing?" the white boy exclaimed, attempting to sound innocent.

"Cracker . . . phone time is up. It's fifteen minutes a call, and your ass done," Daquan said, with his hand still on the holder of the phone.

"Man, you can have this shit!" the white boy said as he dropped the phone and left it dangling.

"Yo, shawty, you got people in line, and I was next!" the black boy named Dre said, with venom in his voice. Unlike 75 percent of the inmates in population, Dre wasn't in fear of Daquan.

Dre was from Valdosta, Georgia, and was built like a farm boy from Mississippi. He stood Daquan's height but had more muscle and had a good reputation for fighting. Quiet and humble, he was waiting for days to bump heads with Daquan.

"Man, listen! Your black ass was in line letting that cracker call back twice. Now you realize that you are in line," Daquan told Dre, whose face frowned up more.

"So you about to just say fuck me, nigga?" Dre asked Daquan, moving in closer to him.

"Call it what you want, nigga!" Daquan retorted before he then turned his back to Dre to dial his home phone.

"Nigga, go ahead and talk to Momma. Just when you get off that phone, come meet me in the paint room. Ain't no reason to put on no act out here in front of everybody. We could get it toe to toe, shawty!"

"I'll do that, no problem, nigga!" Daquan said, tired of hearing Dre give his pre-show talk to him. He watched Dre walk away as his mother answered the phone.

"Hey, baby. How are you?" Renae asked her son.

"I'm okay, Mom. What about you?"

"Daquan, shit's been crazy, Son. People dying every day . . ."

"Who dead now?" Daquan asked.

"Maybe it's not my place to tell you, Son, but you got to know . . ."

"What happen, Mom? Is it Earl? Please don't tell me that!" Daquan exclaimed.

"No, boy! What makes you say Earl, of all people?" Renae asked.

"Because, Mom, I've been having dreams of Earl. You know I don't want to say it."

"Well, don't say it and talk it into existence," she retorted.

"Daquan," Renae sighed, "Yesterday morning, Donavon killed himself."

"What! Where is Shaquana?" Daquan inquired, concerned about his sister and in shock from the news. "What did he kill himself for?" Daquan questioned before his mom could utter a response to his first question.

"Shaquana is stuck in her room. We don't know why he did it. She's talking to us, and Champagne and Brenda are helping her get through it."

"Where's Dad?" Daquan wanted to know.

"Your dad is out and about handling business like usual," she said.

"Can Shaquana come to the phone?"

"Son, right now just let her cool down. I will tell her that you've sent your condolences. Meantime, you have fifteen days left . . ."

Yeah, if I'm not charged with murder before, Daquan thought.

"When you get out of that place, Daquan, you must walk with a clear head," Renae said, something that she told Daquan every time he called home.

"I will, Mom . . ."

"Don't tell me you are, and you don't," Renae said.

"Mom, are you coming this weekend?" Daquan asked his mother, already knowing that she would be there—like every visitation.

"Yeah, boy. Now . . ."

"You have thirty seconds remaining," the operator announced over the phone.

"Okay, Daquan, I love you, and stay out of trouble."

"I will, Mom."

"Thank you for using GTL," the operator announced before disconnecting the call.

As soon as Daquan hung up the phone, he was reminded of what he had had to do for the call. To him, Dre would be another statistic once he knocked him out. With no stops in his stride, Daquan got to the paint room, which was small utility closet big enough for a rumble, something that Dre desperately wanted. There were two lookouts standing at the door so that no one could intervene as the two rumbled. And there were two more at the end of the hallway to alert if a guard came into the vicinity. Dre was already inside the paint room, where the only paint that was ever in the closet was blood. The reason it was called a paint room was to get an understanding across. Dre had his shirt off, which revealed his muscular frame. He had his jumpsuit cuffed at his ankles, and he preferred to rumble barefoot.

I know this nigga from the country . . . ol' Mississippi ass nigga! Daquan thought as he laced his boots tight and loosened his jumpsuit top

Dre just sat patiently waiting until Daquan was suited.

"What's up, nigga?" Daquan exclaimed as he approached Dre with his setup and stood in his infallible stance.

Dre matched his stance with a sui generis set that perplexed Daquan.

What the fuck he think he doing with that? He must think we spiders, Daquan thought.

With unexpected agility, Dre attacked, swinging a wild blow at the head, which barely missed him, which he intended to do to deceive Daquan and his prospect of Dre. Daquan saw the missed shot as an exposure and approached to attack Dre, like he did in every brawl. He knew what he had in the ring with him now. He just had to finish him. Daquan quickly struck Dre with a two-piece, which caused them to clash. Dre ate six grazes and connected with one that made Daquan's knees buckle. As he went down conscious, Dre kneed Daquan in his temple, knocking him out for the count.

"I hope that phone call was worth it!" Dre said as he stepped over Daquan and walked out of the room. He could have taken advantage of him, but he had no traits of a coward to beat a defenseless man.

* * * * *

When Maurice pulled up to the light, one intersection away from his hood, he saw Chad walking out of Wendy's chewing on their fries.

"Busta!" Maurice exclaimed as his adrenaline began to hype up. He was sandwiched in between two cars in the middle lane. "I got to get this nigga," Maurice said as he kept his eyes on Chad, who was now pulling out into traffic beyond the light, going back into their hood. The light turned green, and the traffic began to move.

"I got to catch this nigga before he make it on 3rd," Maurice said to himself as he maneuvered his Mercury through traffic. When he made it to the intersection and turned into the hood, he saw the taillights of Chad's Chevy Impala, and a College Parke police cruiser, sitting on their main strip of MLK Boulevard.

"Damn!" Maurice exclaimed as he turned right on 8th Street.

I'll catch him on the back street. He gotta cross Lincoln, Maurice thought as he accelerated to the corner of 8th, where he saw Chad crossing over to Lincoln.

"Got this nigga!" Maurice said as he reached under his seat and grabbed his Glock .40 while accelerating toward Lincoln Street.

When Maurice turned on Lincoln and 3rd, he was fortunate to see that Chad had pulled up to the Arab corner store.

"Got this nigga!" he said as he passed the store and made a quick U-turn to wait for Chad to come out of the store. There were only a few junkies standing out front, and they were all inebriated and minding their own business. When Chad walked out of the store, he was talking on his iPhone and unaware of his surroundings.

Maurice waited until Chad had walked toward the driver's door before he made his move. Smoothly, he crept up on Chad with his window down and took him by surprise.

Boom! Boom! Boom! Boom!

The shots penetrated his chest, spun him around, and slid him down to his death.

Most of the junkies scattered when they heard the shots, but some stayed to collect the spoils of Chad before it became an official crime scene.

"That's for T-Zoe and the motherfucking 12th, you pooch-ass niggas!" Maurice exclaimed, elated and on the hunt for his next prey of College Park: Romel!

T WENTY-TWO

She heard the shots, his moans, and the junkies stripping him of all his spoils. But she still stood there with the phone to her ears in complete shock.

"What's wrong with you 'Pagne?" Shaquana asked her friend, who looked as if she had seen a ghost. The tears slid down her face inevitably, and that's when Shaquana knew that something was wrong.

"'Pagne! Say something!" Shaquana yelled as she ran up to her and held her.

She'd never seen Champagne in the state she was in, despite seeing her cry plenty of times. They were in Shaquana's room, and Champagne was just walking back into the room on the phone with Chad, about to tell Shaquana goodnight, when she heard the shots over the phone.

"I think that Chad's been shot and killed!" Champagne exclaimed, sniffing from crying.

"What do you mean . . . shot?" Shaquana asked, perplexed.

"I was just on the phone with him and heard it. He's not responding," Champagne retorted.

What is going on? First Donavon kills himself . . . and now Chad's dead! Shaquana thought to herself.

"Champagne, where was he at?"

JACOB SPEARS ~ TRAYVON JACKSON

"At the Arab store in his hood. He only stopped for a second . . ."

"Let's go!" Shaquana ordered as she grabbed her keys and they hastened out the front door. Together, they got into her Audi and drove over to College Park. On their way over, the ride was in complete silence.

"How could this be? Is it for the good or bad?" Champagne asked herself. Just last weekend she found out that she was pregnant, after showing positive on a pregnancy test after missing her period. She knew the chances of the baby being Chad's were slim. But it was the possibility that he had a small chance that left her worried. She loved Chad for how he treated her, and he was always there to talk to about anything. But her heart was taken by someone else who she desired to spend eternity with. She wanted to have all of his kids and marry him.

One day I will . . . if not sooner, Champagne thought.

"Oh my God!" Shaquana exclaimed as she saw the crime scene in front of the store next to Chad's conspicuous Chevy Impala.

Shaquana was too focused on the innumerable cars with red and blue lights and the crime scene investigators to see the smile on Champagne's face, who was unaware of herself smiling unconsciously.

RIP, Chad Davis. It was good while it lasted! Champagne thought as she looked on and pretended to be affected. For Champagne, Chad was just another statistic of what the streets were known to do.

"Are you okay, 'Pagne?" Shaquana asked, looking over at her.

"Yeah! Can we go?" Champagne retorted, putting on her best grief personality.

"Okay," Shaquana answered.

* * * * *

Did Donavon Smith commit suicide because of his transsexual lover ending their nine-month affair, or was he murdered to stay away?

"What the fuck is this shit?" Shaquana exclaimed as she continued to read the Atlanta news on Facebook.

Hollywood's new actor Berlinda Jordan, who's neck and neck with transsexual actor Laverne Cox, was devastated to find out that Donavon Smith . . .

Shaquana was unable to read any more. She vomited on the floor and began crying hysterically. Within seconds, Benjamin and Renae stormed her room.

"Why? Why?" Shaquana cried out.

"Baby girl. What's wrong?" Benjamin asked his daughter out of concern.

"She's pregnant!" Renae said as she observed Shaquana's dinner from last night on her plush pink carpet.

"No, Mom! Nooo! He was a homosexual!" Shaquana yelled out.

"Who, Shaquana?" both Benjamin and Renae said together.

"Donavon! He was a homosexual!"

"Baby, let me handle this," Benjamin told Renae.

"I'm leaving. I love you," Renae said, giving Benjamin a kiss while getting up to leave the room. She was on her way to see Daquan and didn't want to be late.

"I love you too, baby," Benjamin said, letting her leave.

When Renae was gone, Benjamin sat on the edge of Shaquana's bed and said, "Come here, Shaquana."

Finally getting a hold of herself, she crawled over and hugged him.

"Daddy, he tricked me. He never loved me," Shaquana cried out sniffing.

"You're hurt, baby, and I understand that. But please don't let this beat you down. Where are you getting your sources from?" he asked her.

"Champagne texted me and told me to look at the Atlanta News on Facebook. And when I did, this is what I found, Daddy," she said, showing her father the heartbreaking news.

Benjamin was surprised to see that the man he thought was the perfect fit for his daughter was actually a queer living a double life.

But who am I to judge anyone living a double life, when I was out chasing a woman who I loved and barely knew? he asked himself.

"Wow!" Benjamin said after reading the news report.

"It's everywhere in Atlanta, Daddy, which means that it's everywhere in school. And, Daddy, this . . ."

"Will not affect no Clark, baby girl. You'll never know yourself until you give yourself the opportunity."

Speak for yourself, Benjamin Clark, he thought. *Do you know who you are?*

"This means that if you be surprised of anything in life, then you're not ready for the world. And you'll be missing out on life altogether," Benjamin told his daughter.

"It makes sense, Daddy, but the pain is still there," she told him as she wiped away her tears.

"All the men in the world and you mean to tell me that one nigga, who didn't love himself, is preventing you from doing you!" Benjamin jumped from the bed saying. He looked over at his daughter with a frivolous look upon his face that caused her to break out laughing in hysterics.

"Daddy, you so stupid. Why you looking like that?" Shaquana exclaimed.

Seeing his daughter cheer up, he cuddled her in a warm embrace and kissed her on her forehead.

"We are Clarks, baby. We tend to be loving and sometimes impassive. I'm not telling you to give your heart to every man you meet, but until you know what you have, withhold on letting him explore what's in here!" Benjamin told her, softly stabbing her in the chest with his index finger. "To love is to be hurt, and to be hurt is to know how it feels. I don't care how many family members tell you how cute you and a man look. Baby girl, you go off of your own judgment. Because only you know how a man makes you feel," Benjamin told her.

"Thank you, Daddy. What would I do without you?" Shaquana said, giving her father a big hug.

"Young lady! Shaquana Shantrell Clark . . . you'll be a Clark with me . . . and without me!" Benjamin said sincerely. "You hear me, shawty?" he retorted.

"Yes, Daddy! I hear you," Shaquana said, knowing that her dad was a real street nigga and would only give her the game straight from his heart. Being a Clark to Shaquana meant nobility.

There are only a few of us, and that's all it takes to be a Clark. Fuck you, Donavon! The least you could have done was keep it real, Shaquana thought, feeling better and ready to move on—but not love again!

TWENTY-THREE

"The way he sexed me was so amazing. His touches were incomparable to any man I've ever been with. He was able to open my heart and see right through it. From the beginning, I judged him wrong, thinking that he would only want to hurt me—like my past. But I was wrong, and I'm glad to have relinquished to his compassionate healing. He saved me and promised me that no man would ever hurt me again—and I believed him. Together we will make it to the top and enjoy the beats of our hearts. He's my lover and true knight . . . and most of all, the cure to my scars. Who ever thought that danger would become my heart. The look in his eyes is too powerful to resist. His moans are gratification, for he knows that there are no limitations. What we've established is far greater than love at first sight. Damn, I'm so worthy to have this man—a coincident from my past and a fulfillment to my emptiness. I just pray that he is not like the man who has stolen my heart. And that he sees me for what I am—a real queen and ride to die. I'm so grateful to know Mr. Benjamin Clark—my joy and keys to a new start. For without him, I would be stuck in my past—all torn apart."

Staring outside the hotel's windows, she took in the beautiful sight of Atlanta nightlife. Soon she would be at a point in her life where she would know no struggle.

Only a matter of time, she thought as she walked back into the room and crawled back into bed with her lover. She cuddled up against his warm body and lay on his chest. She had a lot of plans, and one of them was to keep him happy.

If I could change anything, it would be nothing! she thought, finally closing her eyes to bring morning sooner than it was to come.

* * * * *

Benjamin had just wired $4.5 million to the first offshore account, when there were two soft knocks at the door. He could still hear Antron recording, and he knew that the staff was gone for the day.

Who the hell is that? he thought as he closed the account data on his desk computer.

"Come in," he called out.

When the door opened, and he saw the gorgeous surprise visitor, and he was more than happy to see the young lady.

"Right on time," Benjamin said to himself, loud enough for her to hear him.

"What's on time?" she said, smiling salaciously.

Benjamin leaned back in his plush, comfortable chair, with his hands locked behind his head and said, "The sweetest Georgia peach, shawty!"

168

"Oh yeah!" she responded as she walked around his desk and climbed onto his lap, with her hands rubbing his chest.

"I hope that you're not upset with me about my unexpected visit, baby. If so, I promise you that I could make it up to you, daddy," she said while unbuttoning his Polo dress shirt.

"Naw, shawty! You okay. I already know that you've missed me. I've . . ."

She cut him off as she placed her lips on his and kissed him both deeply and passionately.

Damn, this bitch is blowing my mind! he thought as he slid his hands up her suede, brown H&M skirt and found her panty-less. He raised her skirt to her hips and removed her Alice + Olivia top, revealing her erect brown nipples.

"Uhh!" she exhaled in ecstasy when he placed his mouth on her nipples. "Benjamin, I love you!" she said, cupping his head as he continued to caress her breasts and suck on her most sensitive spot, other than the sultry mound between her legs. It was times like this when she felt like Beyoncé more than herself—because Benjamin Clark was a man with a blueprint himself.

"I love you too, shawty," Benjamin retorted as he carried her to the leather sofa in front of his desk and made passionate love to her.

* * * * *

"Oh my God! I can't believe this shit!" Shaquana yelled out in frustration at the sound of a blown tire. "It's too damn hot for this shit!" she continued as she pulled over into the entrance of a Perkins restaurant. When she got out to inspect the tire on her front driver's side, it seemed as if the heat had intensified. "Great! Great! Fucking great!" she said while inspecting the rim of the tire.

"I have no clue how to change a damn tire. Dad . . . it seems you forgot to teach me about tires," she mumbled as she tried calling her father, whose studio was just a mile away from her location.

"Pick up, Dad. Pick up!" she said impatiently while tapping her foot and shielding the sun from her face with one of her school folders. When she got no answer, she tried again. But once again, it was to no avail.

"Damn it!" she screamed.

Champagne don't know how to change no tire, but she could come get me, she thought as she dialed her friend's number.

"Hello . . . huh? Yeah, this Champagne. Who is this?"

"This me girl!" Shaquana yelled.

"Well, I can't talk. Leave a message after the beep," Champagne's recorded voice message continued.

"You are stupid!" Shaquana yelled, realizing that she'd been tricked by Champagne's recorded voice as her answering machine had intended to do. Shaquana had forgotten about the answering machine, and it only made matters worse. She was about to call her mom, when she saw the luxurious Range Rover pull up behind her.

Who the hell is this in this nice-ass Range Rover? Shaquana wanted to know. When the doors extended in the air like a Lamborghini and the driver stepped out, Shaquana's heart dropped.

Damn, nigga! Make my day! she thought as the individual approached.

"What's the problem, Ms. Gorgeous?" Maurice said to her as he looked at her flat tire.

"Um, um. My damn flat tire!" Shaquana said, almost speechless and while blushing.

"Damn! All you had to do is tell me to hit it from the back more often. But I guess hitting it again was none of your intentions," Maurice said, being sardonic.

Shaquana caught his curveball and could expect any man to feel the way he felt when all of his calls to her were ignored. She hadn't given him a chance in the world to turn the one-night stand into a sexual or romantic fling.

"I'm sorry, Maurice. But I only intended to let my actions speak. I had a man, and it was wrong for me to do what happened between us."

"At the time you had a man, but what about now?" he asked her, looking into her gorgeous eyes, searching for her honesty.

Shaquana broke eye contact and looked away, trying her best to control her emotions and not let this man see her cry.

But unfortunately, her emotions were far out of her control, and the inevitable tears came, with the comfort of Maurice pulling her into his embrace.

"It's okay, Shaquana, I know you've been hurt. But not every man is the same; although, there are many pit bulls in skirts," Maurice said, getting a laugh out of her.

171

"Thanks, Maurice. But after you fix my tire, can you hold me some more? And I mean somewhere else away from this sun." she said.

Maurice lifted her chin with his hands and planted a passionate kiss on her lips, making her sultry between her legs.

"Anything at your behest, beautiful. But during my inspection, I found a problem," Maurice said.

"And what is that?" she retorted with a pout.

"Your rim is bent, so there's no use in changing a tire," he told her.

"Damn! My dad works down the road. Maybe you could give me a lift, and I'll have him do it," Shaquana said.

Maurice looked at her and thought for a second.

Haitian Beny wanted her father dead by the hands of me, for the blood debt of T-Zoe. Why take a nigga life because another nigga couldn't respect his hustle? From what I've been gathering, the nigga a paid nigga who came a long way to be where he was. T-Zoe, I love you, but not everything is about money. It is something you have to let go, and there is no way I would let Ms. Gorgeous go or hurt her. But I still have a job to do, Maurice thought.

"I'll get you to your dad's safely," he said.

T WENTY-FOUR

I've been doing a million things
neglecting my true main
She my ride or die bitch
far from that Bonny and Clyde shit
We beyond . . .

When Antron saw Shaquana walk through the door with
the Drake-looking nigga, his heart dropped and caused him
to fuck up his ad-libbing to his new track. Through the
window, he could see her giving the guy what seemed like a
tour of the studio.

"We'll run that back in a second. Seems like we have
some distraction!" David, the engineer, said through the mic
from the booth.

"Yeah, we'll do that," Antron retorted as he walked
inside the engineering both and then out another door that
led into the hallway. There he greeted Shaquana and the guy
who had her bruising the dimples in her face from smiling
excessively.

"Hey there, Antron. Sorry to interrupt your recording."

"Naw! Naw, shawty! It's okay. You not intervening in
any kind of way," Antron said in hopes of assuaging any
feelings of discomfort that she might have been feeling.

JACOB SPEARS ~ TRAYVON JACKSON

"Thanks for coming by. Haven't seen you in a while. I see more of 'Pagne than you," Antron said to Shaquana, who missed the understatement.

"Maurice, this is Antron of ATL Money Green Records," Shaquana said, introducing the two men, who both had a serious crush on her.

"Nice meeting you off stage. It's a moment of fan and artist, which I find intriguing," Maurice said, shaking hands with Antron, who seemed disinterested.

It's a sucka behind them Gucci shades, Maurice thought introspectively.

"It's a pleasure to meet ya, shawty," Antron retorted.

"Come, so that you can meet my dad," Shaquana said as she pulled Maurice down the hallway by his arm, seeming happier than ever.

As she walked down the hallway, Antron watched her undulations and all her curves in her leopard mini dress and black Jordans.

Damn! Shawty's ass just spreading every time I see her. I gotta get a taste of that real soon, Antron thought. But he knew deep down that when he did attempt to approach her, he would fall into despondency like every other occasion. Antron adjusted his snap-back Falcons hat and walked back into the booth.

"Thank you, Maurice, for helping me out," Shaquana said as she and Maurice walked toward Benjamin's office.

"It's okay, shawty. I . . ."

"Be quiet!" She stopped abruptly as she listened to the unmistakable sounds of a woman's moans of ecstasy coming from down the hall, close to her father's office.

As she crept toward his office, the moans intensified.

"Baby! I'm cumming, bae. Oh shit!" the unmistakable voice of Champagne moaned out.

I can't believe this shit! Shaquana thought as she shook her head from side to side in disbelief.

"Damn, ma! I think pop's busy. Maybe we can meet some other time."

"No! I'ma beat this ho ass, Maurice. Fuck that!" Shaquana said loud enough for Benjamin and his lover to hear her, because all movement stopped.

"Shawty! You may be upset, but for you to straighten your ol' boy about the next bitch isn't your place!" Maurice said while holding Shaquana firmly around her waist.

Shaquana looked at Maurice with the hurt of a double betrayal from her father and—beyond any doubt—her true best friend. Before the tears had a chance to fall, Maurice caught them with his index finger and wiped them away.

"Let's go, shawty!" Maurice suggested as he turned her from the door and walked away. As they both walked away, Benjamin's door opened and he walked out to see Shaquana and the red boy walking away.

"Damn it!" he said to himself, indecisive on whether he should call her or let her continue to go about her business.

He knew beyond a doubt that she'd heard him and Champagne getting their groove on. Champagne sat up on the sofa with a stomach full of butterflies when she imagined the way Shaquana was feeling.

"Oh my God!" she said, leaning over and vomiting inside Benjamin's garbage can next to the sofa.

Betrayal had a way of hurting some individuals, but it wasn't betrayal of her friend that made her vomit. It was the irrefutable signs of her pregnancy.

"Shawty, you okay?" Benjamin asked.

"She knows it's me!" Champagne stated, wiping her mouth with the back of her hand.

"I know," Benjamin retorted.

* * * * *

A few moments ago she was mirthful while parading Maurice through the studio to meet her dad, until she heard the undeniable moans of Champagne.

I can't believe this bitch! She's supposed to be my homegirl, and all in my daddy's grill, Shaquana thought to herself as she and Maurice walked out of the studio building.

When she searched the parking lot, she spotted Champagne's Honda Accord, hidden behind the Hummer HZ stretch limousine that Antron rode in.

"Baby . . . !"

"Don't baby me, Maurice. She had you just as well. So I don't even know do I feel right about . . ."

"About what, huh? Say it!" Maurice yelled out to her.

"Stipulations and boundaries!" Maurice continued, gesturing quotations marks with his hands.

"And what's that supposed to mean?" she retorted, crossing her arms.

"It means that what we did as three was three, and what we did in the shower was for only two. I have it in me to be a real man to a woman who deserves it . . . and woman, you do! If I'm not bolted down, then there are no stipulations or boundaries," Maurice said to her.

She was touched by how he expressed himself.

"Baby, every man ain't out to hurt you. But I'm sure your daddy told you that you have to give chances to the opportunities," he retorted as he wrapped his arms around her thin waist and embraced her.

Shaquana looked up at Maurice and reached for the back of his head to bring him down to her level. Their mouths found each other as they passionately kissed.

"Give me a chance, shawty," Maurice pleaded, looking into her eyes.

"Please don't hurt me, Maurice," she said.

"You know how it feels, don't you?" he asked.

She thought for a second of what he was asking and then retrospected the moment she'd heard Donavon call out another lover's name in the midst of having sex with her. She could remember the way her heart exploded in her chest— and the many hours that she'd spent crying on the bathroom floor.

She recalled the last time she saw Donavon. He was lying in bed asleep. That thought alone caused her to break down and cry. It wasn't because of the grief or the pain that he had caused her. Shaquana was now crying as she was holding on to the man who she was willing to give a chance at her heart.

"Please, Maurice, don't hurt me!"

"That's easy, shawty! What's hard is intentionally hurting you," Maurice exclaimed, kissing her gently and passionately. "Two things I want you to do," he said.

"What?" she asked.

"Beat her ass and don't be mad at your father, although you have every right to. But that's your mom's place. Much as I hate to say it, men tend to cross boundaries, but we always get caught. No man has yet defeated karma," Maurice said as he walked Shaquana over to his new Range Rover.

* * * * *

Champagne had left, and Benjamin was back into his world of trying to save a woman who he just couldn't find out what it was that made him feel so much for her. One thing he knew for sure was that he refused to let her die. Tomorrow was the deadline for making Jarvis a happy man. He'd just sent the second $4.5 million.

I will not let him kill her nor let him live, Benjamin thought as he closed down his data and left his office for the day. He called Shaquana, only to get no answer. He then checked up on Champagne, who also couldn't get through to Shaquana. She was ignoring all of her calls. One thing that Benjamin was certain about was that Shaquana would not upset her mom and tell her that she'd caught her dad cheating.

My baby is a Clark, and Clarks see no evil, hear no evil, nor speak no evil, Benjamin thought as he drove home to his wife—the sweet woman that he wasn't sure why he cheated on. But at the end of the day, his prospect spoke loud and clear: *When a man or woman chooses to live a double life, the limitations don't exist, meaning that there is nothing to understand about crossing the line. Men and women cross the line just to cross the line. I will talk to my daughter, though nothing needs to be said. Because what's unsaid is understood,* he thought.

"Poor Champagne," he said as he pulled into his driveway

TWENTY-FIVE

Daquan was a young man who could take a loss and who had shown a lot of the other inmates what real courage was. After getting knocked out by Dre, Daquan had awakened to a bigger perspective on life. He gave Dre his props on his unexpected victory against him and continued to go about his day. He and Dre had become close friends and learned so much about each other. The last thing that he would have ever expected was for Dre to be facing the same indictment as he was. Unlike Daquan's story, Dre was a real gunslanger, who had niggas tasting dirt all throughout the hood in Valdosta, Georgia.

One night, Dre and his homeboy had decided to rob an Arab store in their hood. Both he and his boy ran inside incognito with firearms. When the store clerk decided to try his luck and buck the jack, things quickly became incoherent. The store clerk immersed below the counter and came back up with a deadly fusillade from his submachine tommy gun .45. The exchange of fire resulted in Dre backing out of the store, round after round. He was forced to leave his dead homeboy, who the owner took first unexpectedly.

Fortunately for Dre, he was able to escape and body the Arab, who later died from the slugs in his chest from Dre's Glock .40. Now he was trying to dodge an indictment for the murder of his friend and the Arab. The only evidence they had were the tapes and tips from the hood CIs.

Daquan was playing cards when his name was called by one of the guards: "Daquan Clark!"

Dre was his partner, and they both were gambling for tonight's snack, which would be a peanut butter and jelly sandwich. The two white boys that they were playing against had no chance because both Dre and Daquan were cheating on them with body language and code-talking across the table while playing the game Spades.

I wonder what the fuck he want, Daquan thought while continuing to play his hand and ignoring the guard.

"Daquan Clark," the guard yelled again while looking directly at Daquan.

"A couple more days and I'll be done with this shit!" Daquan said as he stood up and simultaneously slammed his remaining cards down on the table, revealing all spades left in the game, which gave them another victory.

"My motherfucking nigga!" Dre exclaimed as he jumped out of his seat exhilarated as he slapped Daquan's hand repeatedly. Both of them did the stanky leg together, causing the entire quad to burst into laughter, including the guards.

"Okay, okay! Let's go, Mr. Clark!" the guard said to Daquan.

"Dre, collect mines, and hold it until I come back . . ."

"Alright, my nigga," Dre retorted.

It wasn't until Daquan walked through the door and was being escorted through the main hallway that the guard then told him why he had called him.

"Daquan, all your property has been stored inside a black bag . . . ," the guard began.

Property stored in a black bag, Daquan thought as he listened to the guard, perplexed.

"You won't be with our facility any longer, Daquan."

"What's going on, sir?" Daquan asked, perplexed as he and the guard walked through the door to intake. When Daquan saw the two familiar detectives, his heart dropped to his nuts and his head began to spin. He knew what it meant when he saw the two detectives again.

"Daquan Coleman Clark . . . I'm here to serve you a capital felony first-degree murder warrant for the murder of Cindy Mendor and Migerle Jean Pierre, which means that you are under arrest . . ."

"And we are here to take you to the big house. Let's try not to have any problems like last time, Daquan," Detective Cunningham added, stepping in to help Detective Barns bring Daquan into custody.

On the ride over to the Jonesboro County Jail, Detective Barns tried every possible technique he could to get a dialogue going between him and Daquan. But Daquan knew better than to talk to the detectives without a lawyer. When he arrived at the jail, he was fingerprinted and processed into the system as an adult. Though he was still a juvenile, murder exempted him from being tried as a juvenile and permitted him to be tried as an adult.

"Keep your head straight, Mr. Clark. Okay, now turn to the left . . . now back to the center. You're doing good. Now turn to the right," the female deputy said, directing Daquan as he took his mug shot and held the numbers AD1327 in his hands.

Damn, I can't believe this shit! They have nothing on me. I killed two devils, not my girlfriend and her damn lover, Daquan thought, thinking of the stupid misconception that got him now facing his life on death row—if convicted.

* * * * *

"Uhh! Shit . . . Benjamin! Yes!" Renae moaned out as Benjamin thrust in and out of her excessive wetness between her legs. They both were fortunate to have the house to themselves. Shaquana was over at a friend's house that neither of her parents had bothered to inquire about.

With her legs on his shoulders, Benjamin was able to penetrate Renae deep and hit her G-spot simultaneously. They had been at it with R. Kelly playing in the background for hours now. He'd made love to her from the kitchen to their bedroom, giving the house a remodel from the last time they had made love, like they were on their honeymoon.

"Baby, I love you!" Renae moaned as she came to her orgasm for the fifth time tonight.

Sweaty and far from tired, Benjamin continued to long stroke her with a deep and powerful penetration. *Damn, this pussy will never go bad!*

"Then why must you cheat?" the voice inside his head asked.

Because Tameka deserves a man in her life, he thought.

"Damn, Benjamin! You fucking the shit out of me!" Renae screamed.

"Arrghhh!" Benjamin groaned out as he exploded inside her as she gripped his love tool with her pussy muscles.

"I love you, baby. Damn, woman!" he exclaimed breathlessly while kissing his wife passionately.

"I love you too, baby," Renae retorted.

"Tomorrow makes twelve years, baby. It's amazing how time could fly by so fast, baby," Renae said, talking about their anniversary.

"Yeah, baby . . . twelve years and more," Benjamin responded.

When he looked at the clock, he saw that it was 2:00 a.m.—and that the hour of saving Tameka had arrived. He would take her from Jarvis and then kill him.

"Come shower with me. I have to get to the club and help Big Dee out. I then have to go handle some business."

"So you're not going to be here in the morning. Is that what you're telling me . . . that you are not going to be a free man on your anniversary?" Renae questioned, with a pout.

"Baby, calm down! I will be free as soon as I'm done handling business. I will not be gone all morning, baby," Benjamin told her while looking into his wife's beautiful eyes.

"Do not mess this day up for us, Mr. Benjamin Clark!" Renae said, pointing her index finger in his face playfully but being dead serious at the same time.

"I won't, baby. Now let's go shower," he suggested as he got up off of Renae and walked into their master bathroom.

Together they assisted each other with washing their bodies and made love once again. After the shower, Benjamin got dressed in an all-black outfit and then headed over to the club to pick up Big Dee.

Tonight it's going to be me and you, homeboy. Just the two of us, Benjamin thought as he pulled into the parking lot of Pleasers.

Before he exited his Jaguar, Benjamin pulled out his iPhone and called Jarvis. The phone rang three times before he picked it up.

"Speak numbers, Benjamin. Because anything else would be a mistake," Jarvis warned him.

Benjamin then reached into his pocket and retrieved the two offshore account numbers and read them off to Jarvis.

"$4.5 million . . . 590-22-662-321 and $4.5 million . . . 590-34-312-222," Benjamin said, now waiting for Jarvis to let him know where to pick up Tameka.

"Good! Good job, Benjamin. Since you did what you were told, I'm going to be straight up with you and let you have this bitch."

Smack!

"Aww!" Tameka screamed out.

"Jarvis, let her go, man. Don't put your hands on her no more. She's paid for!" Benjamin yelled out.

"Benjamin, you want her . . . then come to 1312 Cookerson Road in Savanna, Georgia," Jarvis said, disconnecting the call.

Percy! Benjamin thought as he immediately understood the meaning of it all.

He was going for the big whale. To hit me for $4.5 million a piece was a joke. *Percy is in danger*, Benjamin thought as he called Big Dee.

Big Dee picked up on the second ring and said, "Yo! What's up, big guy?"

"I need you to put T. Jay over the club. We need to leave now. I'm outside. Come. Hurry!" Benjamin yelled into the phone.

He had no way of getting a hold of Percy by phone because the old man distrusted phone lines. The feds paid some agent well just to listen to phone conversations, and Percy knew well of it. He believed that he'd managed to master the dope game because of that principal alone.

"Damn, Percy!" Benjamin exclaimed, praying that his friend wouldn't get hurt.

When he saw Big Dee, he drove toward him and pulled off before Big Dee was all the way inside the car.

"Damn, Percy!" Benjamin continued to stress.

T WENTY-SIX

When she pulled up to the house incognito, she saw that only the kitchen light was on, illuminating the kitchen and partial areas of the living and dining rooms. She discreetly crept over to the side of the house that she knew well, and entered through the den with a spare key that she had made months ago. She quietly closed the door and then instinctively listened to the silence of the home. A moment had passed before she heard her target humming rhythmically to Kem's hit "Promise to Love."

As she heard her descending the stairs, she found a spot behind the den's sofa and squatted in the darkness. A couple seconds later, her target passed the den area mirthfully in satin lingerie and walked into the spacious kitchen.

"Now or never!" the woman who was incognito said as she removed a butcher's knife from the waistband of her black PZI jeans. Maneuvering from her hidden location in the den and into the kitchen was successful. Her target was standing at the kitchen sink rinsing out a glass coffee bowl and still humming "Promise to Love."

With the knife held in her hands in a striking position, she crept up on her prey. Standing less than three feet away, her target spun around with shocking agility and smashed her over the head with the glass coffee bowl, which shattered to pieces, causing her to drop the butcher's knife.

"Bitch!" the masked woman yelled out in pain while holding her head from the blow. She stumbled to the ground and landed on her buttocks.

When she saw her target making a dash for the butcher's knife, she quickly came back to her feet, slightly dazed, and swiped her target's feet out from under her with a swift kick to her ankles.

"Ahhh!" her target yelled out in pain as she fell on her face, banging her head against the tile floor.

The incognito woman quickly jumped on her target's back, grabbed a handful of her hair, and repeatedly rammed her face into the floor.

"Bitch, die! Bitch, die!" she yelled out as she continued to ram her target's head against the tile floor, formulating a pool of crimson blood underneath them both.

Her target was unconscious and felt no pain after the first three times her face was smashed into the kitchen floor. Standing up and getting off her target, she walked toward the butcher knife and picked it up.

"Finish her!" the incognito woman's conscience spoke to her.

"I came here for a reason, bitch!" Champagne said as she stabbed her target repeatedly with the butcher knife, ending her life, all for the love of one.

After sixty-seven stab wounds, Champagne left the bloody kitchen the way her target had come in: mirthfully—humming Kem's song "Promise to Love."

* * * * *

Tittyboo was coming out of the bedroom where he and Shay had just finished making love, when he saw the bright light sweep across the darkness in the apartment.

What the hell is out there? he wanted to know as he walked toward the front door to look out the peephole and get a view of the outside.

A loud impact resounded, followed by the door being taken down with a battering ram. Unfortunately for Tittyboo, he went down with the door.

Boom! Boom!

The explosions of two M84 flash-bang grenades sounded, affecting the hearing ability of every person in the apartment other than the intruders.

"Jonesboro police. Get down on the ground!" one of the officers informed while others swarmed the apartment with their guns drawn.

"Hey, man! What the fuck!" Tittyboo yelled out in pain while lying on his back trapped underneath the door.

"Well I'll be damned! Like a burning house and the cat stuck in the aftermath. Twenty damn years, and I've never seen no shit like this!" Detective Barns exclaimed, getting a good laugh going between him and his raid team.

"Mr. Petway Thorton. You're under arrest, son. Thanks to ya pal Daquan Clark," Barns retorted.

"Man, what the fuck you talking about, cracker?" Tittyboo exclaimed, breathless.

"This is what I'm talking about, nigger!" Detective Barns said as he kicked Tittyboo in the temple with his steel-toe boot, knocking him out cold.

"Get his ass down to the station!" Detective Barns commanded his men.

"And take his bitch in too. Having sex with a minor is against the law!" he retorted, speaking of Shay, who was crying in the bedroom.

"I have kids, mister. I have nothing to do with that girl's murder!" Shay cried out as she was placed in handcuffs.

"Well I'll be damned. You must, because I don't ever recall telling you why I was here. All I said was Daquan!" Detective Barns told her, anxious to get her into the interrogation room on tape and camera.

* * * * *

When Benjamin pulled up to Percy's home, it was just nearing 5:00 a.m. It was extremely dark, as he had expected, and the bushes and lonesomeness made the suspicious atmosphere no better. Benjamin looked around for any signs of threat and felt compelled when he saw nothing.

Damn! This nigga got me by the ears! he thought as he pulled out his iPhone and called Jarvis, who picked up immediately.

"Do us a favor and step out of the car, Ben. And do as I say. You and your bodyguard, Big Dee," Jarvis ordered.

"Man, where is she? I've paid my money, Jarvis. What the . . . !

Click! Click!
Boom! Boom! Boom!

"That's the dog, Benjamin. Does anyone else have to die for something so simple?" Jarvis screamed into the phone hysterically, like a psychotic maniac.

"Fuck, Jarvis!" Benjamin exclaimed to himself. "Okay, man. We're stepping out now," Benjamin said to Jarvis as both he and Big Dee got out of the car and stood in front of it.

"Lift up your shirt and take the weapons from your waist, nigga. Don't forget I know you too well," Jarvis added.

"Yeah, I know. The consequences of making a man out of a boy," Benjamin mumbled to himself.

He did as Jarvis commanded and disarmed himself, tossing both Glock .21s onto the ground, minus the .38 revolver strapped to his ankle.

"Okay, Ben. Hands in the air . . . and walk toward the house slowly," Jarvis commanded Benjamin.

"What now? You gonna cheap-shot me, shawty?" Benjamin asked Jarvis.

"If I wanted you dead, Benjamin, I would have had you boxed and carried away," he told him. "Now, let's get on with this! I plan to be in Mexico by the time the sun comes up, so I can enjoy my share of retirement," Jarvis informed.

With this hands and iPhone extended in the air, Benjamin began to walk toward Percy's front porch, which completely dark. Benjamin took four steps before a strong muscular arm wrapped around his neck and had him in a half nelson, making him incapable of resistance. It didn't take Benjamin long to realize that Big Dee was the perpetrator.

"Deee!" Benjamin managed to let escape from his mouth, attempting to unwrap the muscular arm from around his neck. But unfortunately for Benjamin, his strength slowly left him, making him feeble. Darkness soon overtook him as his body went limp, for he was now unconscious.

Big Dee picked him up and threw him across his shoulders, finally carrying him into the house. He passed Tameka, who was holding the door open for Big Dee to walk through.

* * * * *

"Yes, Jerome, baby. I know exactly what you mean," Brenda said as she pulled up to her sister's house, like she did every morning. She was on the phone with her man, Jerome, who was planning to visit for the weekend from Canada. "Baby, you know . . . I can't wait to see you. I've been having this scratch lately on my kitty."

"Ohhh shit! Change of plans. Sounds like someone's STD positive."

"Boy, shut up and stop playing. You know what I mean, boy!" she joked as she stepped out of the car, slowly closing her door with her ghetto-fabulous booty. She then began to walk toward the front door, in no hurry.

"So, when is Earl coming?" Jerome asked.

"Next week, baby, and I want to go ahead and finally sit the both of ya'll down. He's my son, but he will respect my love life . . . and who I choose to accept in my life," Brenda explained to Jerome.

"Most definitely, baby!" he retorted.

"Baby, I miss you so much."

"And I miss you too, boo!" Jerome answered.

"Hold on! This tramp might be in here sleeping," Brenda exclaimed as she stuck her key inside the doorknob, unlocked it, and walked into the house.

"Renae, girl! You up or what?" Brenda screamed into the house while closing the door behind her.

She got to be asleep, Brenda made of the still silent surroundings as she walked toward the kitchen.

"Re . . . !"

When Brenda saw the bloody shoe print, she froze in her tracks and surveyed the kitchen.

What the hell is this? she thought as she followed the trail to the other side of the island, where she came upon her sister's dead body on the floor, beneath which was a tremendous pool of blood.

Brenda dropped her iPhone on the kitchen tile in panic and cried out loud.

"Noooo! Renaeeee! Lord . . . why?"

Brenda fell to her knees and embraced her sister's lifeless body in her arms.

"She's dead! Renae is dead!" she continued to sob.

EPILOGUE

When Benjamin had gained consciousness, he found out quickly that his hands were tied behind his back with a rope, and he was sitting at a table with five family faces. Only four of them were slamming dominoes and drinking Seagram's gin from plastic cups. There was an old school classic from Marvin Gaye emanating from Percy's antique turntable.

"Well I be damned, shawty. Look who's finally here to join us. Baby, come pour our dear friend a drink," Jarvis said as he looked over at Benjamin while sipping from his cup of orange juice and Seagram's.

"Okay, baby," the distinct voice from Tameka answered from behind him.

What the fuck is going on? Benjamin thought, perplexed as he stared at Jarvis, Haitian Beny, Big Funk, Corey, and Big Dee sitting around the table.

"So this is what it boils down to, huh? I treated every one of ya'll like family, all to be crossed, huh!" Benjamin exclaimed, expressing how he truly felt.

"Well, partner. You knew what it was when I told you, shawty. I gave you a chance to get on the right side of the road. But you continued to be stubborn. Ben, sometimes you have to pay attention to your team players' considerations, other than yourself," Haitian Beny said.

"Here's your drink, sir," Benjamin heard Tameka say as she came up from behind him and dashed a cup of Seagram's in his face.

"Bitch!" Benjamin yelled out to Tameka.

Smack!

"No . . . you're the bitch!" Tameka screamed after slapping Benjamin in his face.

Benjamin watched with fire in his eyes as she walked around the table and sat in Jarvis's lap. Her face was battered like he'd last seen her at his house.

"Tameka! Why?" Benjamin asked, feeling sick to his stomach.

"No, it's Majik to you," she answered, pulling the mask from her face to reveal a much better, beautifully healed face, despite having a black eye from her boyfriend, who Benjamin had killed in her apartment.

"Thanks for killing that bastard boyfriend of mine and having Marie care for me . . ."

"He always knew how to pick the best. That I could say about him for sure," Mrs. Marie exclaimed, walking into the kitchen. She rubbed Benjamin's head like he was a handsome young child again and pinched his cheeks, causing the gang to explode into laughter.

He was far from feeling humiliated. He was hurt from betrayal, and only had himself to blame. It was times like this that made him appreciate his wife, but he was afraid that it was too late to gratify his love for his true beloved.

"I kind of liked you, Benjamin. But you were far from being my type once I found out who you truly were . . . a married man with no heart for a woman. How could you really think that we would possibly be together when you have a wife and Ms. Champagne? And how could you cheat Antron out of all that money that he could be making? Well, that's okay, because he'll have a new contract come next week," Tameka began. "Benjamin . . . two things that I don't play about are my heart and money," Tameka continued as she kissed Jarvis passionately on his lips for all to see.

"Where's Percy?" Benjamin asked, wondering what his part was in the conspiracy.

"Where's King Solomon?" Haitian Beny responded, with a question to answer Benjamin's question.

"I once was your brother's keeper, but now I'm your grim reaper," Jarvis said, coming from under the table and aiming a Glock .40 at Benjamin's chest and squeezing the trigger repeatedly until the clip was empty and the barrel left smoking.

Boom! Boom! Boom!

"Well, let's get to Mexico, beautiful," Jarvis said to Tameka, caressing her face and then kissing her again on her lips. "Because we have a honeymoon to celebrate."

After Big Funk and Corey poured gasoline throughout Percy's house and set it aflame, the gang left the house together. They were even richer than they ever intended to be, after finding Percy's millions in the bathroom under the tub, where they left Percy's body with his dog, Spot.

Never the End

Stay tuned for:

Two Masks: One Heart II
Forever a Clark

BOOKS BY GOOD2GO AUTHORS

GOOD 2 GO FILMS PRESENTS

THE HAND I WAS DEALT- FREE WEB SERIES
NOW AVAILABLE ON YOUTUBE!
YOUTUBE.COM/SILKWHITE212

To order films please go to *www.good2gofilms.com*

Name:_____

Address:_____

City: _____ State: _____ Zip Code: _____

Phone:_____

Email:_____

Method of Payment: Check   VISA   MASTERCARD

Credit Card#:_____

Name as it appears on card: _____

Signature: _____

Item Name	Price	Qty	Amount
48 Hours to Die – Silk White	$14.99		
A Hustler's Dream - Ernest Morris	$14.99		
A Hustler's Dream 2 - Ernest Morris	$14.99		
Business Is Business – Silk White	$14.99		
Business Is Business 2 – Silk White	$14.99		
Business Is Business 3 – Silk White	$14.99		
Childhood Sweethearts – Jacob Spears	$14.99		
Childhood Sweethearts 2 – Jacob Spears	$14.99		
Childhood Sweethearts 3 - Jacob Spears	$14.99		
Childhood Sweethearts 4 - Jacob Spears	$14.99		
Flipping Numbers – Ernest Morris	$14.99		
Flipping Numbers 2 – Ernest Morris	$14.99		
He Loves Me, He Loves You Not - Mychea	$14.99		
He Loves Me, He Loves You Not 2 - Mychea	$14.99		
He Loves Me, He Loves You Not 3 - Mychea	$14.99		
He Loves Me, He Loves You Not 4 – Mychea	$14.99		
He Loves Me, He Loves You Not 5 – Mychea	$14.99		
Lost and Turned Out – Ernest Morris	$14.99		
Married To Da Streets – Silk White	$14.99		
M.E.R.C. - Make Every Rep Count Health and Fitness	$14.99		
My Besties – Asia Hill	$14.99		
My Besties 2 – Asia Hill	$14.99		
My Besties 3 – Asia Hill	$14.99		
My Besties 4 – Asia Hill	$14.99		
My Boyfriend's Wife - Mychea	$14.99		
My Boyfriend's Wife 2 – Mychea	$14.99		
Naughty Housewives – Ernest Morris	$14.99		
Naughty Housewives 2 – Ernest Morris	$14.99		
Never Be The Same – Silk White	$14.99		

Stranded – Silk White	$14.99		
Slumped – Jason Brent	$14.99		
Tears of a Hustler - Silk White	$14.99		
Tears of a Hustler 2 - Silk White	$14.99		
Tears of a Hustler 3 - Silk White	$14.99		
Tears of a Hustler 4- Silk White	$14.99		
Tears of a Hustler 5 – Silk White	$14.99		
Tears of a Hustler 6 – Silk White	$14.99		
The Panty Ripper - Reality Way	$14.99		
The Panty Ripper 3 – Reality Way	$14.99		
The Teflon Queen – Silk White	$14.99		
The Teflon Queen 2 – Silk White	$14.99		
The Teflon Queen 3 – Silk White	$14.99		
The Teflon Queen 4 – Silk White	$14.99		
The Teflon Queen 5 – Silk White	$14.99		
The Teflon Queen 6 - Silk White	$14.99		
The Vacation – Silk White	$14.99		
Tied To A Boss - J.L. Rose	$14.99		
Tied To A Boss 2 - J.L. Rose	$14.99		
Tied To A Boss 3 - J.L. Rose	$14.99		
Time Is Money - Silk White	$14.99		
Two Mask One Heart – Jacob Spears and Trayvon Jackson	$14.99		
Two Mask One Heart 2 – Jacob Spears and Trayvon Jackson	$14.99		
Two Mask One Heart 3 – Jacob Spears and Trayvon Jackson	$14.99		
Young Goonz – Reality Way	$14.99		
Young Legend – J.L. Rose	$14.99		
Subtotal:			
Tax:			
Shipping (Free) U.S. Media Mail:			
Total:			

Make Checks Payable To:
Good2Go Publishing
7311 W Glass Lane,
Laveen, AZ 85339